MANTISSA

MANTISSA

JOHN FOWLES

JONATHAN CAPE
THIRTY BEDFORD SQUARE LONDON

First published in 1982
Reprinted 1982
Copyright © 1982 by J. R. Fowles Ltd

Jonathan Cape Ltd, 30 Bedford Square, London WC1

A short extract from *Mantissa* was first published in the
magazine *Antaeus* in 1981.

British Library Cataloguing in Publication Data
Fowles, John
Mantissa.
I. Title
823'.914[F]   PR6056.085

ISBN 0-224-02938-X

Printed in Great Britain by
Butler & Tanner Ltd
Frome and London

Then, carefully examining what I was, and seeing that I could pretend that I had no body, that no outer world existed, and no place where I was; but that despite this I could not pretend that I did not exist; that, on the contrary, from the very fact that I was able to doubt the reality of the other things, it very clearly and certainly followed that I existed; whereas, if I had stopped thinking only, even though all I had ever conceived had been true, I had no reason to believe that I might have existed – from this I knew that I was a being whose whole essence or nature is confined to thinking and which has no need of a place, nor depends on any material thing, in order to exist. So that this I, that is to say the soul by which I am what I am, is entirely distinct from the body, is even easier to know than the body, and furthermore would not stop being what it is, even if the body did not exist.

René Descartes, *Discours de la Méthode*

SYLVIA: We must be serious now. My stars say I shall marry a man of distinction, and I'll look at nothing less.

DORANTE: If that were me I'd feel threatened, and go in fear of proving your horoscope. I'm an atheist over astrology

SYLVIA: ... but a profound believer in your face.

SYLVIA: (*to herself*) What a pest he is! (*to ANTE*) Will you stop this? What's it matter to you that my destiny rules you out?

DORANTE: It didn't predict that I wouldn't fall in love with you.

SYLVIA: No, but it said it wouldn't do you one bit of good, and I can tell you it's right. You are capable of talking about something else besides love, I presume?

DORANTE: From the moment you're capable of not inspiring it.

SYLVIA: Really, this is outrageous, I'm going to lose my temper. Once and for all, will you stop being in love with me!

DORANTE: If you will stop being.

Marivaux, *Le Jeu de l'Amour et du Hasard*

I

They were generally represented as young, beautiful, modest virgins, were fond of solitude, and commonly appeared in different attire, according to the arts and sciences over which they presided.

Lemprière, under Musae

It was conscious of a luminous and infinite haze, as if it were floating, godlike, alpha and omega, over a sea of vapour and looking down; then less happily, after an interval of obscure duration, of murmured sounds and peripheral shadows, which reduced the impression of boundless space and empire to something much more contracted and unaccommodating. From there, with the swift fatality of a fall, the murmurs focussed to voices, the shadows to faces. As in some obscure foreign film, nothing was familiar; not language, not location, not cast. Images and labels began to swim, here momentarily to coalesce, here to divide, like so many pond amoebae; obviously busy, but purposeless. These collocations of shapes and feelings, of associated morphs and phonemes, returned like the algebraic formulae of schooldays, lodged in the mind by ancient rote, though what the formulae now applied to, why they existed, was entirely forgotten. It was conscious, evidently; but bereft of pronoun, all that distinguishes person from person; and bereft of time, all that distinguishes present from past and future.

For a while a pleasing intimation of superiority, of having somehow got to the top of the heap, still attached to this sense of impersonality. But even that was soon brutally dispersed by the relentless demon of reality. In a kind of mental somersault it was forced to the inescapable conclusion that far from augustly floating in the stratosphere,

9

couched as it were in iambic pentameters, it was actually lying on its back in bed. Above the eyes presided a wall-lamp, a neat, rectangular, opaque white plastic panel. Light. Night. A small grey room, a pale grey, the colour of a herring gull's wing. Eternal limbo, at least eventless, tolerably nothing. If it had not been for the two women staring down.

Obscurely reproached by the closer and more requiring face, it made another unwilling deduction: for some reason it was a centre of attention, an I of sorts. The face smiled, descended, with a mixture of the solicitous and the sceptical, concern tainted with a perhaps involuntary suspicion of malingering.

'Darling?'

With another painfully swift and reducing intuition it realized it was not just an I, but a male I. That must be where the inrushing sense of belowness, impotence, fool-ishness came from. It, I, it must be he, watched the mouth glide down like a parachutist and land on his forehead. Touch and scent, this could not be film or dream. Now the face hovered over his. Whispered words issued from the red orifice.

'Darling, you know who I am?'

He stared.

'I'm Claire.'

Not at all clear.

'Your wife, darling. Remember?'

'Wife?'

The most strangely alarming yet: to know one has spoken, but only by the proximity of the source of the sound. The brown eyes hinted at appalling depths of con-jugal betrayal. He tried to attach word to person, person to self; failed; and finally shifted his eyes to the younger and more distant woman on the other side of the bed – who smiled as well, but professionally and indifferently. This person, hands in pockets, trimly observant, wore a white medical coat. Now her mouth also gave birth to words.

'Can you tell me your name?'

Of course. Name! No name. Nothing. No past, no whence or when. The abyss perceived, and almost simultaneously, its irremediability. He strained desperately, a falling man, but whatever he was trying to reach or grasp was not there. He clung to the white-coated woman's eyes, abruptly and intensely frightened. She came a step or two closer.

'I'm a doctor. This is your wife. Please look at her. Do you remember her? Do you remember having seen her before? Anything about her?'

He looked. There was something expectant in the wife's expression, and yet hurt, almost peeved, as if its owner resented both the stupidity of the procedure and his silent stare. She looked nervous and tired, she wore too much make-up, the air of someone who has put on a mask to prevent a scream. Above all she demanded something he was not able to give.

Her mouth began to announce names, people's names, street names, place names, disjointed phrases. Some were repeated. He had perhaps heard them before, as words; but he had no idea what relevance they were supposed to have, nor why they should increasingly sound like evidence of crimes he had committed. In the end he shook his head. He would have liked to close his eyes, to have peace to reforget, to be one again with the sleeping blank page of oblivion. The woman bent closer still, scrutinizing him.

'Darling, please try. Please? Just for me?' She waited a second or two, then glanced up. 'I'm afraid it's no good.'

Now the doctor leant over him. He felt her fingers gently

widen his eyelids, as she examined something about his pupils. She smiled down at him as if he were a child.

'This is a private room in a hospital. You're quite safe.'

'Hospital?'

'You know what a hospital is?'

'Accident?'

'A power cut.' A hint of dryness enlivened her dark eyes, a merciful straw of humour. 'We'll soon have you switched on again.'

'I can't remember who . . .'

'Yes, we know.'

The other woman spoke. 'Miles?'

'What miles?'

'Your name. Your name is Miles, darling. Miles Green.'

The faintest flit of an alien object, a bat's wing at dusk; but gone almost before it was apprehended.

'What's happened?'

'Nothing, darling. Nothing that can't be cured.'

He knew that was wrong; and that she knew he knew. There was altogether too much knowing about her.

'Who are you?'

'Claire. Your *wife*.'

She spoke the name again, queryingly, as if she began to doubt it herself. He looked away from her to the ceiling. It was odd, yet soothing; gull-grey, yes, gulls, one knew gulls; lightly domed, and quilted or padded into small squares, each of which was swollen out, pendent, with a little cloth-covered grey button at its centre. The effect was of endless upside-down rows of miniature but perfectly regular molehills, or antheaps. Somewhere, in the momentary silence, a sound obtruded, the hitherto unnoticed ticking of a clock. The doctor leant over him again.

'What colour are my eyes?'

'Dark brown.'

'My hair?'

'Dark.'

'Complexion?'

'Pale. Smooth.'

'How old do you think I am?' He stared. 'Have a guess.'

'Twenty-seven. Eight.'

'Good.' She smiled, encouragingly; then went on in her briskly neutral voice. 'Now. Who wrote *Pickwick Papers*?'

'Dickens.'

'*A Midwinter Night's Dream*?' He stared again. 'Don't you know?'

'Midsummer.'

'Fine. Who?'

'Shakespeare.'

'Can you remember a character in it?'

'Bottom.' He added, 'Titania.'

'Why do you remember those two in particular?'

'God knows.'

'When did you last see it acted?'

He closed his eyes and thought, then opened them again and shook his head.

'Never mind. Now – eight times eight?'

'Sixty-four.'

'Nineteen from thirty?'

'Eleven.'

'Good. Full marks.'

She straightened. He wanted to say the answers had come from nowhere, that being mysteriously able to answer correctly only made incomprehension worse. He tried feebly to sit up, but something constrained him, the tight way the bedclothes were tucked in; and a volitional weakness, as in nightmares, where wanting to move and moving are aeons, or an eternal baby's cot, apart.

'Lie still, Mr Green. You've been under sedation.'

His secret alarm grew. Yet one could trust those alert and intent dark eyes. They held the muted irony of an old friend of the opposite sex – completely detached now, yet still harbouring the ghost of a more affectionate interest. The other woman patted his shoulder, reclaiming her share of attention.

'We must take it easy. Just for a few days.'

He reluctantly transferred his look to her face; and derived from that 'we' an instinct to displease.

'I've never seen you before.'

She laughed, a little noiseless gust, as if she were amused, he was so preposterous.

'I'm afraid you have, my dear. Every day almost for the last ten years. We're *married*. We have children. You *must* remember that.'

'I don't remember anything.'

She took a breath, slightly bowed her head, then glanced again across at the doctor, who he now sensed shared, though it was veiled behind her bedside manner, his growing dislike of this implication of blame, or moral imperative. The woman was too anxious to establish an ownership of him; and one has to know who one is to wish to be owned. He felt an overwhelming desire to be inviolable: an object she might pretend to possess, he could not fight that, but not her tame pet to prove it. Best to regain the nothingness, the limbo, the grey, ticking silence. He let his eyelids fall. But almost at once he heard the doctor's voice again.

'I'd like to start some preliminary treatment now, Mrs Green.'

'Yes, of course.' He caught the wife-face making a simper across the bed, woman to woman. 'It's a relief to know he's in such good hands.' Then, 'You will let me know at once if . . . ?'

14

'At once. Don't worry. This first disorientation is quite normal.'

The woman, his alleged wife, looked down at him, still unconvinced, still tacitly accusing. He realized, but with irritation, not sympathy, that she was flustered, without a recipe for such situations.

'Miles, I'll be in again tomorrow.' He said nothing. 'Please try and help the doctor. Everything's going to be all right. The children are missing you.' She tried one last appeal. 'Jane? Tom? David?'

Her voice was almost wheedling, and made them sound more like overdue bills, past follies of spending, than children. She took another small breath, then bent and pecked him on the mouth. I plant this flag. This land is mine.

He did not watch her leave, but lay looking up at the ceiling, his hands by his sides beneath the bedclothes. The two women spoke by the door in low voices, out of sight. Sedation. Power cut. Anaesthetic. Operation. He shifted his feet, then felt for the side of his legs. Bare skin. He felt higher. Bare skin. A door closed, the doctor was back beside him. She reached and pressed a bell-stud beside the bed, and scutinized him for a moment.

'You must try to understand it's a shock for them as well. People don't realize how much they rely on recognition as a proof they exist. When things like this happen, they feel scared. Insecure. Right?'

'I've got nothing on.'

She smiled briefly at the non sequitur; or perhaps at the notion that loss of clothes was more shocking than loss of memory.

'You don't need anything. It's very warm. Much too warm, in fact.' She touched her own white tunic. 'I wear nothing under this. They keep the thermostat so high,

15

we've all complained about it. And not having any windows.' She said, 'You know what a thermostat is?'

'Somehow.'

He craned a little, looking for the first time round the room. There was indeed no window, and hardly any furniture, no more than a small table and a chair in the far left-hand corner from where he lay. The walls were grey-quilted like the domed ceiling. Even the door opposite the foot of the bed was quilted. Only the floor had been spared, in some attempt to lighten the monotony of the rest: it was carpeted in a dull flesh-pink, the tone painters once called old rose. Quilting, padding, prison: the connection escaped him, but he sought the doctor's eyes, and she must have guessed what he lacked words for.

'For silence. The latest thing. Acoustic insulation. We shall move you out as soon as you start picking up.'

'Clock.'

'Yes.' She pointed. It hung on the wall behind him, near the corner to his left, an absurdly fussy and over-ornamented Swiss cuckoo-clock, with an alpine gable and a small host of obscure shapes, peasants, cows, alpenhorns, edelweiss, heaven knows what else, carved on every available brown wooden surface. 'It was left us by a previous patient. An Irish gentleman. We thought it added a human touch.'

'It's awful.'

'It won't disturb you. We've disconnected the striking mechanism. It doesn't cuckoo any more.'

He remained staring at the hideous clock: its lunatically cluttered front, its dropped intestines of weights and chains. It did disturb him, standing for something he feared, he couldn't say why; an anomaly, an incongruous reminder of all he could not remember.

'Was he cured?'

'His was rather a complex case.'

He turned his head and looked up at her again. 'He wasn't?'

'I'll tell you about him when you're better.'

He digested that. 'This isn't ... '

'Isn't what?'

'Mad people?'

'Heavens no. You're as sane as I am. Probably saner.'

Now she sat on the edge of the bed, her arms folded, turned slightly towards him, as they waited for the bell to be answered. Two pens and a thermometer case were clipped inside an upper pocket of her tunic. Her dark hair was bound severely back at the nape, she wore no make-up; yet there was something elegantly classical about the face, of the Mediterranean. The skin was very clear, a warmth hidden in its paleness, perhaps she had Italian blood; not that she did not seem perfectly English in manner, obviously of well-bred, even upper class, background, the sort of young woman whose intelligence had made her choose a serious profession rather than live in idleness. He wondered if she were not after all Jewish, a scion of one of those distinguished families who had long combined great wealth with scholarship and public service; then wondered from where on earth he could even wonder that. She reached a hand and patted the side of his body, to reassure him.

'You're going to be fine. We've had far worse.'

'It's like being a child again.'

'I know. The treatment may not work at once. We must both be patient.' She smiled. 'So to speak.' She stood and pressed the bell again beside the bed, then resumed her seat.

'Where is this?'

'The Central.' She watched him. He shook his head. She glanced down, said nothing for a moment, then looked at him with one of her quick quizzes. 'I'm here to get that memory of yours back into circulation. You search. Everyone knows the Central.'

He sought; and in some peculiar way knew both that the seeking was a waste of time and that there was something wise in not trying. It was not so unpleasant, after the first shock, this total severance from all one was or might be: to be not expected to do anything, to be free of a burden, forgotten in its kind, but deducible by its absence – a weight one had never seen, yet one's mental back felt relieved. Above all there was the restfulness of being in this coolly competent young woman's hands and care. A delicate neck and throat showed in the discreet V of the white tunic.

'I wish I could see my face.'

'I'm your mirror. Just for now.'

He consulted it, and saw nothing distinct at all.

'I haven't been in an accident?'

She looked grave. 'I'm afraid so. You've been turned into a toad.' Slowly, by something in her eyes, he realized he was being joked out of too much self-alarm. He managed a wan smile. She said, 'That's better.'

'Do you know who ... what I was?'

'*Am.*'

'Am.'

'Yes.'

He waited for her to go on. But she watched him in silence: another test.

'You're not going to tell me.'

'You're going to tell me. One day soon.'

He was silent for a moment or two.

'I suppose you're a ... '

'A what?'

'Couches. You know.'

'Psychiatrist?'

'That's it.'

18

'Neurologist. Abnormal brain function. My special field is mnemonology.'

'What's that?'

'How memory works.'

'Or doesn't.'

'Sometimes. Temporarily.'

Her hair was tied at the nape by a wisp of scarf, the only feminine touch about her clothes. The ends showed an alternate pattern of tiny printed roses and detached elliptical leaves, black on white.

'I don't know your name.'

She turned towards him on the edge of the bed and slipped her thumb under the left lapel of the tunic. There was a small plastic name-strip: DR A. DELFIE. But then, as if revealing even this tiny bureaucratic detail about herself was unclinical, she stood.

'Oh where *is* that nurse.'

She went to the door and looked out; in vain, since she returned once more beside the bed and pressed the bell, long and insistently this time. She glanced down, her mouth wryly pressed, exonerating him from any blame over her impatience.

'How long have I been here?'

'Just a few pages.'

'Pages?'

She had folded her arms, and yet again there was the ghost of a quiz in her watching eyes. 'What should I have said?'

'Days?'

She smiled more openly. 'Good.'

'Why did you say pages?'

'You've mislaid your identity, Mr Green. What I have to work on is your basic sense of reality. And that seems in good shape.'

'It's like losing all one's luggage.'

'Better luggage than limbs. As they say.'

He stared at the ceiling, struggling to reconquer a past, a place, a purpose.

'I must be running away from something.'

'Perhaps. That's what we're here for. To help you dig back.' She touched his bare shoulder. 'But the thing now is not to worry. Just relax.'

She moved once more to the door. It was strangely dark beyond, he could see nothing. He stared at the domed and quilted ceiling, its forest of little hanging pods, each with its end-button. For all their greyness they were breastlike, line after line of schoolgirls' breasts, a canopy of nippled buds. He felt like pointing this out to the doctor, but she remained waiting in the open door; and then an instinct told him it was not something he could say to a woman physician. It was too personal, too whimsical, and might offend her.

At last the doctor turned. Someone came quickly in behind her: a young West Indian nurse, white cap and brown face over a starched blue-and-white uniform. In one hand she carried a coiled red cylinder of rubber sheeting. She rolled her eyes at the doctor.

'Sister on the warpath. For a change.'

The doctor gave a resigned nod, then spoke down to him.

'This is Nurse Cory.'

'Nice to have you with us, Mr Green.'

He made a sheepish grimace up at the nurse.

'Sorry.'

She raised a mock-stern finger; a flash of brown eyes, a rich Antillean voice.

'Now no sorry. Else you get smacked.'

A pretty girl, a humour, a jolly bossiness. By some rare coincidence in what otherwise must have been very different racial genes, her eyes were exactly the same colour as the doctor's.

'Close the door, nurse, would you? I want to do the primaries.'

'Sure.'

Once again Dr Delfie had her arms folded, in what was evidently a favourite pose. Her gaze down at him seemed for a moment to be curiously speculative, as if she had not yet fully made up her mind what his treatment should be; as if she saw him less as a person than a problem. But then she gave a small smile.

'They won't hurt. Many patients find them pleasantly relaxing.' She glanced across at the nurse, who had returned to the other side of the bed. 'Okay?'

They stooped and with a familiar expertise eased up the mattress first on one side, then on the other. The bedclothes were released and in a quick series of folds stowed away to the end of the bed. He tried to sit. But the two were at once back beside him, forcing him firmly but gently down again.

Dr Delfie said, 'Lie still. Just as you are.' Though quiet, her voice was markedly more brisk; and she read his embarrassment. 'My dear man, I'm a doctor, this is a nurse. We see naked male bodies every day of our lives.'

'Yes.' He added, 'Sorry.'

'Now we have to put a rubber sheet under you. Turn towards me.' He turned, and felt the sheet laid close along his back by the nurse. 'Now the other way. Over the roll. That's right. Good. On your back again.' He stared up at the quilted ceiling. The sheet was pulled taut beneath him. 'Now raise your arms and put your hands under your head. Like so. Good. Now close your eyes. I want you to relax. You're in the best hospital in Europe for your problem. We have a very high success rate. You're not lost any more, you're on the way to recovery already. Just relax all your

muscles. And your mind. Everything's going to be fine.'
There was a pause. 'Now we're going to test for certain
nervous reactions. You must lie quite still.'

'Yes.'

He kept his eyes obediently closed. There were a few
moments more of silence, only the ticking clock, then the
doctor said quietly, 'Right, nurse.'

Two light hands touched the underside of the arms
cocked back on the pillow, ran down to the armpits, then
down his sides; stopped at the hip-bones, pressed down on
them.

'My hands nice and warm, Mr Green?'

'Yes thank you.'

The nurse removed her hands, but only momentarily.
One of them deftly lifted his limp penis and laid it back
and rested on it; while the fingers of the other hand en-
circled his scrotal sac and began to massage it slowly. His
eyes opened in alarm. The doctor leant over him.

'The memory nerve-centre in the brain is closely
associated with the one controlling gonadic activity. We
have to check that the latter is functioning normally. This
is standard procedure. No reason to feel shy. Now please
– close your eyes again.'

In her eyes there was no longer any humour or dryness
at all, only medical seriousness. He closed his own again.
The scrotal massaging continued. The other hand began to
stroke the exposed underside of the penis. Though he did
not feel relaxed at all, the manipulation did seem merely
clinical, a routine matter; and as if to confirm it, the doctor
spoke across the bed and his body to the nurse.

'Have they done anything about that sluice yet?'

'You're jokin'.'

'I don't know what it is about Maintenance. The more
you complain, the longer it takes.'

'All that lot do is play gin rummy in the boiler-room. I seen 'em.'

'I'll try to get Mr Peacock to chase them.'

'Best of luck.'

He guessed, from behind his closed eyes, that the doctor liked the young nurse's sarcastic resignation; that they smiled at each other after that last remark. There was a silence. The gentle squeezing continued, and the stroking, with now and then a little rolling by the fingers. Yet something about the words they had spoken nagged at him. He seemed to recall that snatch of hospital shop, to have lived it before, even this before ... yet how could he have, and not remembered?

The doctor murmured. 'Reaction?'

'Negative.'

He felt the penis, still limp, lifted and allowed to fall; then the manipulation recommenced. Desperately now, through the fog, the cruel grey wall of amnesia, he tried to regain the lost structure of experience and knowledge. Hospitals, doctors, nurses, medicine, treatments ... there was a movement on the doctor's side of the bed.

'Give me your right hand, Mr Green.'

Frozen, he did nothing, but the doctor took the hand from beneath his head and led it upwards. It touched a bare breast. Once more shocked and horrified, he opened his eyes. Dr Delfie was leaning over him, with the white tunic open, staring at the wall above his head, as if she were doing no more than take his pulse. His hand was led to the other breast.

'What are you doing?'

She did not look down. 'Please don't talk, Mr Green. I want you to concentrate on tactile sensation.'

His eyes wandered down the opening of the white coat,

and then up again, in a third access of astonishment, to her still averted face. He had not taken literally the remark about wearing nothing.

'I don't know what you're trying to do.'

'I've just told you. We must test your reflexes.'

'You mean ...'

She looked down with a distinct touch of impatience.

'You must have had to produce specimens during past examinations. This is no different.'

He pulled his hand away. 'But I ... you ...'

Her voice was suddenly strict and cold. 'Look, Mr Green, Nurse and I have many other patients to attend to. You do want to be cured, don't you?'

'Yes, of course, but –'

'Then close your eyes. And for goodness' sake try to be a little more erotic. We haven't got all day.' She leant across him, supporting herself on either side of the pillow. 'Now both hands. Anywhere you like.'

But he kept his hands where they were, back on the pillow.

'I can't. I don't know you from Adam.'

The doctor took a breath.

'Mr Green, the person I want you not to know me from is Eve. Or are you trying to tell me you'd rather have this treatment from a male nurse and doctor?'

'I take exception to that.'

She stared sternly down. 'Do you find my body repellent?' Her voice and eyes were peremptory now, brooking no refusal. He glanced down from the face to the shadowed breasts, then turned his head aside.

'I can't see what this has got to do with –'

'What you call "this" happens to be the most up-to-date and approved method for your condition.'

'I've never heard of it.'

'A few minutes ago you'd never heard of your wife and children. You are suffering from severe memory-loss.'

'I'd have remembered this.'

'Can you remember your politics?' He said nothing. 'Your religious beliefs? Your bank balance? Your profession?'

'You know I can't.'

'Then you will kindly trust me to know what I'm doing. We don't undergo long years of training in my particular specialism in order to have our professional judgement questioned – and above all on such silly grounds. You're in perfectly good physical health. I examined you thoroughly yesterday. Your genitalia are quite normal. I'm not asking for the impossible.'

He remained with his head turned away; then swallowed and spoke in a lower voice.

'Couldn't I . . . on my own?'

'We're not testing your ability to produce mere *sperm*, Mr Green.'

There was something he did not grasp about the contemptuous emphasis she gave 'sperm', as if it were synonymous with scum or froth.

'It's so embarrassing.'

'You're in a hospital, for heavens' sake. There's nothing personal in this. Nurse and I are simply carrying out standard practice. All we ask is a little co-operation. Nurse?'

'Still negative, doctor.'

'Now no more nonsense, Mr Green. I have a perfectly ordinary female body. Shut your eyes and use it.'

Her voice and look were like nothing so much as those of a nanny, of the old school, admonishing a dilatory infant to perform another natural process.

'But why?'

'And will you *please* stop asking these pointless questions.'

She looked away at the wall behind the bed, forbidding any further discussion. In the end he closed his eyes and gingerly raised his hands to find the hanging breasts. He did not caress them, but merely held them. They were in themselves warm and firm, pleasant handfuls; and he became aware of a faint tarry fragrance, like that of myrtle-flowers, no doubt from some antiseptic soap she used. But he was much less conscious of the doctor's femininity than of an anger inside himself. At least he knew he must very recently have undergone a severe trauma, that his mind must be in a particularly delicate and fragile state – and here they were, not only taking gross advantage of his weakness, his still partly drugged condition, but (far worse) disregarding totally any moral feelings he might have.

To his acute dismay, for Nurse Cory had not stopped her ministrations, he felt the beginning of an erection. Perhaps the nurse made some silent signal to the doctor, for she spoke in a slightly less carbolic voice; rather that of a Minister of Tourism addressing a delegation of foreign travel agents, and obedient to a hopeful text, composed by some civil servant who had never actually met a foreign travel agent in the flesh.

'Now I suggest you explore other regions of my body.'

It was too much. He let his hands fall back on the pillow, though he kept his eyes shut.

'This is obscene.'

Dr Delfie was silent a moment, then, exhibiting a much less pleasant aspect of her socially and intellectually superior background, curtly and coldly incisive.

'If you must know, Mr Green, your memory-loss may well be partly caused by an unconscious desire to fondle unknown female bodies.'

He opened his eyes in indignation.

'That's a totally unwarranted assumption!'

'On the contrary, it has every warrant. Monogamy is a biological nonsense, a mere transient accident of history. Your true evolutionary function, as a male, is to introduce your spermatozoa, that is, your genes, into as many wombs as possible.' She waited, but he said nothing. She went on in a lower voice. 'I repeat. Run your hands elsewhere.'

He sought for something in her eyes: the faintest trace of humour, of irony, of humanity even. But there was none. She was implacably indifferent to his scruples, his modesty, his sense of decorum. In the end he shut his eyes and found the breasts again, then felt cautiously upwards to the delicate throat, to the angles where the neck joined the shoulders; then down to the breasts again, to the sides, the curved indent of the waist, with the light linen of the opened tunic on the backs of his hands. The doctor shifted, and raised a knee on to the side of the bed.

'Anywhere you like.' His right hand moved inwards; stopped. 'Come on, Mr Green. You've touched the pubic area before. It won't bite you.'

He withdrew his hand.

'That's another thing. What about my wife?'

'Mrs Green is fully aware of the nature of this treatment. I explained it to her before you woke up. I have her signed consent in my office.'

One ancient fact, a merciful ally, suddenly blew back into his consciousness. He opened his eyes again, and stared up accusingly into hers.

'I thought there was a thing called the Hippocratic Oath.'

'A doctor shall use all the means in his or her power to cure the patient in care. If I remember.'

27

'Proper means.'

'The proper means is the most efficacious means. Which is what you are getting.'

The nurse's invisible hands would give him no peace. He looked a moment longer into the doctor's eyes, then found he could not bear their now quite overt irritation and disapproval. He once more closed his own. After a moment Dr Delfie crouched lower over him. A nipple touched his lips, then again, and the scent of the myrtle-flowers was stronger, evoking in some lost recess of mind sunlit slopes above azure seas. He opened his eyes, in twilight now, tented beneath the sides of the tunic; once more he was invited to suckle the insistent breast. He twisted his head to one side.

'Brothel.'

'Excellent. Anything that spurs your libido.'

'You're no doctor.'

'Bonds. A whip. Black leather. Whatever you fancy.'

'This is monstrous.'

'Would you like Nurse to undress?'

'No!'

The doctor withdrew a little.

'I do hope you're not a racialist, Mr Green.'

He kept his head averted. 'I demand to see the doctor in charge.'

'I am the doctor in charge.'

'Not when I get out of here. I'll have you struck off the register.'

'I trust you've noticed that already you are searching far less for words. So perhaps there is –'

'Go to hell. Piss off.'

There was a silence. The doctor's voice became even icier.

'You may not be aware of this, Mr Green. But all resorts

to the imagery of defecation and urination are symptoms of culturally induced sexual guilt and repression.'

'Bugger off.'

There was yet another silence. Then the nurse spoke.

'We lost it, doctor.'

He heard an impatient outbreath from Dr Delfie; a hesitation, then she took her knee from where it rested and stood by the bed.

'Nurse, I'm afraid there's nothing for it. We'll have to do a PB.'

There was a rustle of fabric. He gave a newly alarmed look from the pillow, to see the doctor, who had taken off her tunic and now stood quite naked, hand it across the bed to the nurse. She glanced down at him with an equally naked vexation.

'You're only getting this because you're a private patient, Mr Green. I can tell you now I wouldn't tolerate your behaviour if you were on the National Health. Not for a moment.' She folded her arms. 'Quite apart from anything else there is a considerable waiting-list for beds in this ward. We work under great pressure.'

He summoned his strength and braved her eyes.

'What's a PB?'

'A plexicaulic booster.' She glanced impatiently back at the door. 'Nurse, do please hurry up. You know what a case-load I have today.'

Nurse Cory had, during this exchange, gone to the door and hung the white tunic on a hook there. She had not turned back, but unpinned the front and unfastened the back of her apron, and hung that up as well. Now she was absorbed in unbuttoning her blue dress. At the doctor's voice she hastened the task, slipped the dress down her brown arms, and placed it over the apron; crowned the hook with her cap, slipped out of her shoes. She walked

29

back, supplely and lightly, as naked as the doctor, to her side of the bed. He stared, both mesmerized and panic-stricken, at the dark and the light female bodies. They were the same height, though the twenty-year-old nurse was not so slim; nor so clinical, for he thought he detected a certain sardonic amusement in her look down at him, in the ghost of a pout that haunted her mouth. The doctor spoke again.

'Before we begin I think I had better inform you that your obstinacy may not be quite so moral as you imagine. We are by no means unfamiliar here with patients who resist treatment because they hope we shall be forced to employ perverted practices ... so called. We do very occasionally apply them in cases of genuine and persistent erotic recalcitrance. But never at an early stage like this. So if you are secretly attempting to drive us to coenonymphic or pseudoterguminal stimulation, I can tell you now – no chance. Is that clearly understood?'

'I don't even know what they are, for God's sake.'

'And the same applies to the Brazilian fork.'

'Or that!'

This brought another brief silence. The doctor assumed the look of a schoolmistress who knows she is being deliberately provoked to lose her temper. Her hands went to her hips.

'And one last thing, Mr Green. We also take the dimmest possible view of crypto-amnesia.' She paused, to make sure the warning had registered. 'Now on your side. Facing me.'

The nurse's hand slipped under his left shoulder, coaxing him round.

'Go on, Mr Green. Mrs Grundy says. Be a good boy.'

He cast a suspicious and resentful look at the smiling West Indian face, but eventually turned on his side. With a neatness of movement and simultaneity of timing that suggested considerable experience his two medical attendants were immediately on the bed as well, on their respective sides. Nurse Cory lay against his back, while the doctor disconcertingly pressed her back against his front. He felt them both squirm a little, respectively forwards and rearwards, as if to secure him more firmly in the vice of their two bodies. A gratuitous wriggle of the black girl's loins against his bottom, as she did this, confirmed what he had already suspected about her. He stared at the doctor's dark hair, the wisp of scarf an inch or two from his nose. There was a brief silence. Then the doctor spoke. Her voice was quieter, in an evident, but not entirely successful attempt to make a less peremptory approach.

'Right. Now kindly place your left hand on my breasts.'

She lifted an arm towards the ceiling. He hesitated, but then did as he was told; as one might, at the behest of a driving instructor, place one's hand on some knob or switch. The doctor lowered her arm. Her hand came to rest on his, to keep it where it lay.

'Now listen closely, Mr Green. I will try to explain one last time. Memory is strongly attached to ego. Your ego has lost in a conflict with your super-ego, which has decided to repress it – to censor it. All Nurse and I wish to do is to enlist the aid of the third component in your psyche, the id. Your id is that flaccid member pressed against my posterior. It is potentially your best friend. And mine as your doctor. Do you understand what I am saying?'

He felt Nurse Cory kiss, then lick, the nape of his neck.

'This is an infamous abuse of personal privacy.'

'I'm afraid that is your super-ego speaking. This procedure bears some resemblance to mouth-to-mouth resuscitation, just as amnesia is akin to drowning. Do you follow me?'

He stared at her hair. 'Under the very greatest protest.'

She took a breath, though her voice remained deliberately neutral and matter-of-fact. 'Mr Green, I'm bound to tell you that I expect this kind of attitude in the culturally deprived. But not in patients of your background and education.'

'Moral protest.'

'I cannot pass that. Your mind is where I need help.'

'I may for the moment not know who I am. But I'm damn sure it wasn't someone who'd have ever –'

'Forgive me, but that is hardly a logical statement. You don't know who you are. There is therefore an equal mathematical possibility that you were sexually promiscuous. Statistically I can reveal that it is rather more than an equal chance. In your particular social grouping and profession. Which latter is one, I must also warn you, that has an extremely long and well-recorded history of general incapacity to face up to the realities of life.'

'That bloody woman did tell you something!'

'A good deal less than your hostile attitude to her.'

'I couldn't remember who she was, that was all.'

'But you appeared to prefer looking at me. Even though you no more knew who I was.'

'You seemed more understanding. Then.'

'And more attractive?'

He hesitated. 'Perhaps.' He added, 'Physically.'

'In common parlance, you fancied me?'

'I'm a very sick man. Sex was the last thing in my mind. And for God's sake tell this nurse to stop nibbling at my neck.'

'Would you prefer the attentions of her mouth elsewhere?'

He was silent a moment.

'That's revolting.'

'Why, Mr Green?'

'You know perfectly well why.'

32

'No. I don't know why.'

'My dear woman, I may have forgotten facts. I have not forgotten common decency. If I had, I should almost certainly have strangled you by now.'

She pressed his passive hand a little closer against her breasts. 'That's precisely my puzzle, Mr Green. Why your apparently violent dislike for our methods manifests itself only in words.'

'I don't know what you mean.'

'You've made no attempt to push us away, to get off the bed, to leave the room. All actions of which you are capable. And which would appear to be the normal physical equivalents of your state of mind.'

'It's not my fault if I'm half drugged.'

'Ah. But you aren't, Mr Green. You may have felt so at first waking. But you only woke because I had given you a counter-sedative. A stimulant. It would have taken full effect long before now. You can't put it down to that, I'm afraid.' He felt like someone in a chess game, trapped without warning. The doctor pressed his hand again. 'I'm not criticizing you, Mr Green. Merely asking.'

'Because ... because I can't remember anything. I presume someone knew what they were doing when they sent me here.'

'Are you saying you concede it is possible our methods do have their reasons?'

'It's your manner I can't stand.'

The doctor did not answer for a moment; then she quietly removed his hand from her breast, shifted away a little, and turned round on her other side to face him. Her eyes were so close that he had difficulty in focussing them properly, but something in them, and her face, suggested that she realized he was not to be further bullied. For once it was she who lowered her eyes. She spoke in a near-whisper, almost as if she did not want Nurse Cory, just behind him, to hear.

'Mr Green, our work here is not easy. We are not totally devoid of ordinary human feelings. There are patients who ... well, that frankly we can relate to more easily than others. I shouldn't be saying this, but when I examined you on admission, I did not, as I confess I sometimes do at that stage, secretly wish that I had followed my original ambition of specializing in paediatrics. As a matter of fact I have been looking forward to working on your case, partly because I anticipated from certain features special to it that you would be eager yourself to work on it in conjunction with me. Inasmuch as a patient can, that is. I sincerely beg your pardon if I counted too much on that prognosis. On the other hand I hope you will believe that no one can work in this ward who does not put patients' health well above personal feeling. Who has not learnt to sacrifice extramural notions of modesty and privacy on the greater altar of human need.' Her eyes rose gravely to meet his. 'I trust you can accept at least this?'

'If I must.'

'Mr Green, in a moment or two I shall close my eyes. I would like you to kiss me, then to turn round and kiss Nurse. Purely as a symbol of our common humanity in a situation that is difficult for all three of us. Then perhaps we can all make a fresh start and help you achieve the erection, and eroticism, I know you are capable of.'

Before he could answer she had tilted her mouth a little; no longer the doctor, the schoolmarm, or even a grown woman – but most of all like a demure and obedient niece waiting for a kiss from an uncle. He felt a pressure from his back, discreetly urging him to do what was asked. He looked at the face so close to his own, the dark eyelashes resting on the pale skin, the classical nose, the finely proportioned mouth. In other circumstances one might have called it a beautiful face, rather divinely balanced between intelligence and a latent sensuality. He wavered, still resisted, felt unfairly trapped. But he had to do something. He craned forward, touched his pressed lips briefly against hers, and drew back immediately.

'Thank you, Mr Green.' Her eyes opened, the medical persona reappeared. 'Now I'm sure you're not a racialist, but you were less than kind to Nurse Cory just now. In case the fact is lost along with the rest of your memory, perhaps I may remind you of the very considerable West Indian contribution to the efficiency of our hospital services. I'm sure Nurse would appreciate it if you would turn and extend the same token of understanding to her.'

She eased her body back a little, and he felt the body behind do the same. Dr Delfie's severely professional eyes held his, and perhaps it was above all to escape them that he finally turned. He kept his arm rigidly along the side of his body, as if he were standing to attention. Nurse Cory's hand came up to his shoulder. Her eyes were also closed, the fuller mouth tilted up in the same waiting, submissive, childlike manner. However, her body seemed warmer, more curved and pliant than the doctor's; and though she lay quite still, he sensed a dormant agility.

He bent his head to deliver the second token of understanding. But this time he did not encounter the same passivity. The nurse's hand slipped up behind his head. Their mouths had barely lost contact after his quick peck than they met again. Her lips opened a little, and he detected the same tarry fragrance as with the doctor. It must have been used in mouthwash as well as soap, and by all the staff. A moment or two passed, he tried to draw back, but the hand behind his head insisted he should not, and the girl's body strained closer. Her tongue began to probe. Then a dark leg bent and slipped up across his, bringing them closer still.

He felt no less horrified, shocked and indignant than before, but somehow still lacked the will to push the persistent young nurse away. After all, she was a comparatively innocent party; and there was even a certain pleasure in putting the doctor's nose out of joint by being more co-operative with her junior. He had not been mistaken over the agility, for now the lithe and restless creature bore him backwards on the pillow and swarmed half across him, seemingly not to be denied this demonstration of her ability to prolong and deepen a kiss. In another few moments she had managed to find her way entirely on top of him. The doctor must have got off the bed. He felt the nurse reach down and catch his limp wrist on the rubber sheet, then lead his hand to lie on the rounded contour of her right cheek. To the now quite unashamedly suggestive synec-doches of her tongue were added quiverings and tremulous little borings in the surface beneath his hand. In a vain attempt to calm her he raised his right hand and placed it on the other cheek.

He knew, as in a nightmare, that he was slipping fatally towards disaster; and equally was powerless to prevent it. Yet somewhere inside his blinded psyche an entire moral being continued to protest at this abject surrender to animality, this blatant pandering to the basest instincts. It was seconded by an aesthetic being, a person of taste, a true if temporarily lost Miles Green – who would not, he knew it in his bones, have ordinarily been caught dead in such vulgar and humiliating physical circumstances, or for a moment listened to the doctor's specious justifications. It occurred to him, with a dawning excitement, that this intuitive sense of what he could never have been might be a useful clue to what he actually was, and he began to speculate – with some difficulty, as Nurse Cory had now raised herself on her arms and was teasing his face and mouth with her exuberant young breasts – as to a suitable profession. Almost at once he had evidence that he was on the right track, and that the doctor, in hinting at something vaguely louche, promiscuous, had once again been deliberately misleading him.

From nowhere, miraculously, came a first recall of something he knew was autobiographical, and to do with his occluded past. Though it was only the very haziest apprehension, without detail, he knew it had something to do with rows of watching, attentive faces; and that what they were watching was he himself. Of that he was quite sure. Indeed in his excitement at this breakthrough he inadvertently dug his nails into the nurse's bottom, a gesture she misinterpreted, so that he had to suffer a paroxysm of breasts and loins in response. The last thing he wished was to be distracted from his train of thought. It therefore seemed wisest to encourage her in hers. Having improved his grip on the exposed cheeks, and undergone another bout of trembling, he was able to concentrate anew on his discovery.

More specific clues his crippled memory refused to surrender; but he felt convinced that he had been used to performing in some way in public. As he absentmindedly caressed an excited nipple with the end of his tongue, purely to still the body on top of him, he tried to evoke a suitably senior and respected profession. It was obviously something far removed from the frivolity of the arts, from mere entertaining – the law, perhaps. The Church did not feel quite right. A public-school headmaster was a possibility, or the Navy. Captain Miles Green, RN, had a very plausible sound – yet brought no more precise and clinching echo. It crossed his mind that the theatrical profession might just, after all, fit the bill, since there did seem something spellbound, as also something half hidden in darkness, about this blurred, yet definite, sense of an audience. On the other hand actors were not socially responsible people, as he felt more and more certain the true Miles Green was.

For what his equally blurred yet definite real self rose against, as abruptly as Nurse Cory herself, suddenly erect, a knee on the bed on either side of his chest, was the idea that it would, in its right mind, ever have allowed any of this to happen. A further inspiration breathed upon him. Was it not actually most likely, he thought, as the black girl, having seized his hands, now led them up, like lifeless flannels or sponges, over her smooth stomach to ablute the cones of dark-tipped flesh above, that he was a Member of Parliament? A determined opponent of the forces of evil and permissive morality in society?

And what had the wretched doctor said about inability to face up to the realities of life? Was not that just the sort of snide, childishly malicious remark the general public liked to make about their elected representatives? He felt a thrill of intuitive certainty that he was very warm ... and then another thrill, for something else she had said still worried him. Why indeed had he not left the room at once? But wait: suppose he truly was a Member, stumbled on a flagrant medical malpractice of import far beyond the walls of this one hospital? Then it was clear. Between personal repugnance and public duty, there was only one choice, as Gladstone had so amply witnessed in his work with prostitutes.

Gladstone – he had remembered Gladstone! He felt a third *frisson* of incipient self-discovery; for not only the memory of Gladstone, but that of more recent public figures selflessly braving the sex-hells of Hamburg and Copenhagen on behalf of their constituents returned to him. He felt profoundly relieved. Albeit unconsciously, he had, in not leaving this room, chosen the right, the responsible thing, and was doing what he began to feel sure he was elected to do.

If that were so – my God, a day would come when he would arraign doctor, hospital, treatment, all, in terms that would settle their hash for good. Now a hand was led down and invited to explore between the splayed thighs of the kneeling nurse. No silent Member, he: he would catch Mr Speaker's eye and rise, nothing could stop him rising, with aplomb and dignity and full force, to his most solemn and convincing height. 'Is the Minister aware of the increasing incidence of gross sexual abuse of mentally incapacitated patients by nymphomaniacal and multiracial members of staff in a certain major hospital? Does he realize that their hapless victims . . .'

Alas, further composition of his speech became impossible, for Nurse Cory's attention must have been caught by something else rising behind her. Her hand released his, felt back.

'Mr Green! You done it!'

The next moment she had sunk upon him. His mouth was briefly but violently kissed, then she seemed to writhe and slither down his body, like a snake. He felt his own nipples being licked, and gave up trying to imagine how this appalling scene might end.

'That's enough, nurse. Nurse!'

The nurse lay still, at the second and sharper admonition, her cheek couched against his stomach. He opened his eyes. Dr Delfie was standing by the side of the bed, her arms folded, eyeing her prone assistant with more than a hint of the disapproval hitherto reserved for him. Nurse Cory raised herself from body and bed, then stood with her head bowed.

'Sorry, doctor.'

'How many times do I have to tell you we use the Hopkins-Sezscholsky sequence here?'

'I forgot.'

'That's the third time this week.'

'It did work, doctor.'

'It's not a question of what works. I'm talking about ward rules. It's for your own protection, nurse. As I keep telling you, over-stimulation just doubles our work-load. That's why we insist on Hopkins-Sezscholsky. You know that.' She added, not without a touch of the sanctimoniousness of those who like to pull rank, 'I don't want to have to speak to sister.'

Nurse Cory looked across the bed in horror. 'Oh please don't, Dr Delfie. Please. I got the old cow up to here already.'

'Nurse, you also do *not* speak like that about senior staff in front of patients.'

The nurse bowed her head again. 'It's only what most of them say.'

'That's not the point.'

'Honest, I'll never do it again, doctor. Cross my heart.'

Dr Delfie softened a little. 'Very well. But I don't want to have to speak to you again.' At last she diverted her look back and down to their patient, with a very thin smile of token apology. 'Do forgive me, Mr Green. Nurse is still under training here.' Then she looked down at the middle of his body. 'Now. Let's see how the sensible part of you is doing.'

He felt her weigh and assess the size and rigidity of the sensible part. He closed his eyes.

'See if you can't make it a shade bolder still. Just another

40

centimetre.' The part was tapped underneath. 'Splendid. Again. Again. Once more. Fine.' Her voice had acquired a new tone: it was almost one of praise, with even a hint of surprise. She stood over him again. 'I'll complete treatment myself today, as it is our first session. But generally it will be done by the nurses. I shall of course come and check progress from time to time. All right?'

He opened his eyes, but he was beyond words, and could answer only with a baleful stare; which she ignored. Without warning, her left knee was on the bed and then, with an easy athletic movement, she had straddled across him on all fours.

'Nurse will perform the insertion.'

Still he could only stare, unbelieving of what was happening, even as it happened. He felt the doctor, suspended on her arms, expertly lower her loins, camber, arch, adjust herself. Insertion. He was cased, sunk, buried deep.

'I hope that's not too uncomfortable?'

Still he stared. She seemed to have gained yet another personality. There was no irritation or impatience now, merely a quiet concentration. She spoke again, oblivious of his look and all it tried to express. 'Your hands on my breasts, please.'

He closed his eyes. Something made his hands rise and find the breasts.

'That's the spirit. Try and delay your orgasm. Purely for your own sake. I shan't have one.' She began to rock slowly up and down, still suspended on her arms. The pubis lingered a moment, held down against his own. 'I wish to retain you as long as possible, so please say if you find this motion over-stimulating.' He pressed his lips together, determined not to speak. There passed half a minute or so of a slow lumbar rising and falling. 'That's very good. Nicely sustained.'

He opened his eyes, driven beyond endurance.

'I don't know how you can even *think* of doing a thing like this.'

She gave him a condescending and cursory smile down. 'I expect that's because you're not scientifically trained, Mr Green.'

'Like a woman of the streets.'

'I'm afraid you'd find very few modern sociologists who did not see prostitutes as serving a most useful function.' Again the pubis pressed and lingered before it withdrew. 'For a start, the incidence of rape would be much higher without them. There is also abundant evidence that they relieve a great deal of personal and therefore community stress in other ways.' She stopped the movement at their loins. 'Now we'll rest for a moment.'

He let his hands drop.

'That's exactly what this is. Rape. The other way round.'

'Oh come now, Mr Green. You're not going to suggest that just because I have temporary possession of a few medically and biologically already obsolescent inches of your anatomy ... I thought that childish old male phobia was confined now to only the most primitive societies.' He closed his eyes. 'I'm not half your physical strength. A mere naked woman, Mr Green.'

'I had realized that.'

'I think you would realize it better if you opened your eyes and put your hands to more effective use. I should like you to see and feel my defencelessness. How small and weak I am, compared to you – how rapable, as it were.' He did not budge. 'Mr Green, I don't wish to sound vain of my skills, but I've worked long enough in this ward to know that your reluctance to give way to perfectly natural instincts is most unusual. One reason I can already detect is that you are over-attached to the verbalization of feeling, instead of to the direct act of feeling itself, which in turn means that –'

'For God's sake – who's doing all the talking?'

Now her voice assumed a tone of intolerably prim – were the adjective not so ill-descriptive of physical circumstances – knowingness.

'I talk only to explain. Also to see if your erection confirms your hostile verbal attitude. I am glad to note that it does not.'

'It would if I had anything to do with the accursed thing.'

She smiled.

'You really are quite a case, Mr Green. Castration anxiety. Now fear of pleasure. I think we shall have to have you stuffed and put in a museum.'

'I can tell you one pleasure I look forward to immensely – not paying your bill.'

'Mr Green, there's no need for all this – unless of course your threats make you feel even more sexually excited than you already are, in which case do please continue. We are well aware here that for some men the notion of copulation is inseparable from the notion of defilement, owing to an unresolved –'

'I can tell you another thing. That nurse knows a damned sight more about the handling of patients than you do. At least she did her bit with some warmth. You're the one who needs a few lessons.'

He had hoped to ruffle the doctor, but when she spoke it was in the same insufferably official, detached, superior voice.

'I have already explained why I can show no feelings whatever for you, Mr Green. I'm afraid you must get used to that. So, incidentally, must Nurse Cory. That is why I spoke to her. Our sole function is to provide you with a source of erotic arousal. In anything in that area – in the domain of coital technique – you have only, within reason and depending on the availability of staff, to ask, and we will do our best. If you would prefer some other position, we can offer most of those in the *Kama Sutra*, Aretino, the *Hokuwata Monosaki*, Kinsey, Sjöstrom – that is, except the Brazilian fork, as already mentioned – Masters and –'

'You know something? You're about as erotic as a bloody iceberg.'

'Thank you for mentioning that, Mr Green. I'm a great believer in full patient participation in therapy. I see some balancing oral treatment is indicated.'

Before he could answer, her arms bent and she sank on him. He did make a last-moment attempt to push her away, but it was too late. Half a minute later she propped herself up on her elbows, just over his face. His eyes now had something obscurely stunned and patently puzzled about them. He tried to plumb the dark-brown irises above, but without success.

'There, Mr Green. I hope that shows our clinical method does not preclude at least some mutual concession to erogenous reality.' She glanced down at his mouth, then bent and gave it a last small kiss. 'I think you're going to be one of my best patients.' She pushed up on her arms again. 'Now let's see if we can provide a climax to match. Nurse, are you ready?'

'Yes, doctor.'

He glanced sideways, and saw the now uniformed Nurse Cory rise from the chair by the table in the corner where she had been sitting, and come towards them. He felt Dr Delfie contract her vaginal muscles.

'That's excellent, Mr Green. Well done. Now I shall increase the tempo slightly. If you'd put your hands on my hips. Good. Grip me as firmly as you like. I want you to set the rhythm.' The increased tempo began. 'Don't try to force it. Just time the thrusts. Delay as long as you can.' Her hanging head bent further, as she looked down to where their bodies were joined. 'Lovely. Relax ... thrust. All you have, Mr Green. Relax, thrust. Again. A good steady rhythm, that's the secret. Super. And again. A little faster. From deep as you can. Splendid. Push with your whole body. Keep the rhythm. It's better for you, it's better for your baby.'

'My baby!'

But the doctor seemed too absorbed in her therapy to answer now. He looked desperately at Nurse Cory, standing beside the bedhead.

'What does she mean – baby?'

The nurse raised a finger to the lips. 'You jus' concentrate, Mr Green. Won't be long now.'

'But I'm a man, for God's sake!'

The nurse winked. 'So enjoy it.'

'But –'

Dr Delfie's voice cut in.

'Please stop verbalizing, Mr Green.' She was beginning to breathe deeply, and had to pause between each sentence. 'Now. One last effort. I can feel it coming. Good. Good. Splendid. With the hips. Hard as you can.' Her head remained bowed, apparently intent on the ever more forceful and accelerating movement of their loins. 'There we are ... there we are ... perfect. Perfect. Safe as houses. Keep going, don't stop. Right to the very last syllable. Nurse!'

He was vaguely aware of Nurse Cory moving to the end of the bed – out of his sight, since the energetic doctor, still suspended on her arms, blocked his view.

'One last push. One more. One more. One last one.'

There was a little gasp from her, as if she were the one who had really given birth; then an abrupt cessation of movement. A silence. He was conscious of Nurse Cory moving back to the corner of the room. The doctor's head remained bowed, the ends of her scarf hanging down. She was taking urgent breaths, like someone who has dived too deep. Then she slumped down on him. Her skin was damp with perspiration, he could feel her heart pounding. But the collapse was clearly an aftermath of physical effort, not emotion, since she averted her head.

For half a minute or so he stared at the ceiling, in a state of delayed shock. He had not managed, at the end, to stay as fully objective as he would have wished, but he had not been so far gone as not to remark some strange words, or misconceptions . . . the terrible thought swept over him that despite her denial he was indeed in a lunatic asylum, a mental institution, and had somehow fallen into the hands of two other patients through some oversight of the proper medical staff. But what on earth would he be doing in such a place? And how could it be left so slackly superintended?

He looked surreptitiously across the room at the nurse. She sat with her back half turned away from him, bent over something at the table, papers, no doubt the file of his case. She did not suggest madness at all; if anything, so intently did she now stop and read some passage of a report, she revealed an unexpectedly studious side. Nor did the body under whose weight he lay seem anything but unmistakably normal. There was no sobbing, no wild cackles of glee. In some odd way he found the doctor's silence, her obvious exhaustion, rather touching; and as one might want to comfort a woman miler who has run her heart out, even though she has failed to win (since recall of anything beyond his profession – and even that, he felt, had to rest a high probability rather than certainty – remained tantalizingly out of his reach), he let his arms come belatedly round her back and held her lightly embraced.

He reflected, in the comparative peace, and ticking

silence. Perhaps there was, behind the Freudian jargon, some truth in what the doctor had said, some clinical backing. On second thoughts, he might do better not to be too quick with a Parliamentary speech of denunciation and exposure. Further research was clearly advisable. After all, a decent modern politician's prime duty is not to expose the wrong, but never in any circumstances to be caught in it.

His eyes once more drifted across the room to where Nurse Cory's neatly uniformed body still sat busied over his file. Her delicate brown hands, the slim dark calves and ankles beneath the hem of the starch-blue skirt ... if his did prove to be a difficult case, as he began to have a presentiment that it was, then he must accept the likelihood of a long course of treatment, and take it like a man. He experienced an anomalous desire to murmur something to that effect into the hair beside his cheek, but somehow it seemed a shade premature. One had to consider one's future position. However, he patted the doctor's moist back in a mildly fraternal sort of style, by way of a tacit and at least partial apology – to say that he acknowledged she had done her best, even though she had lost.

The doctor did not respond. He had a suspicion that she had momentarily dozed off. He did not mind; if anything he was further, if still somewhat reluctantly, touched. It showed she was human after all. The weight of her slim and well-shaped body, almost as well-shaped as that of Nurse Cory, was not disagreeable. One could hardly say one had, in the circumstances, landed on one's feet; but one might, it began to dawn, have done worse. One felt rather pleasantly exhausted oneself, now one came to think of it, and distinctly less worried about the loss of memory.

He closed his eyes, but a sound made him open them again. Nurse Cory had risen from the table, and was knocking and shuffling her papers together. She turned, gay and jaucy, recovered from her dressing-down, and came back towards the bed; her eyes on him, cradling the papers she had been sorting.

'Hey, Mr Green, who's a clever boy? Who's in luck?'

'What luck?'

She came a step or two closer, beside the bed, and gazed down at the small sheaf of paper crooked in her right arm; then smiled coyly and roguishly up at him.

'It's a lovely little story. And you made it all by yourself.'

He stared uncomprehendingly at her inanely sentimental grin down at him. The doubts he had dismissed flooded back. He was in a psychiatric hospital, the girl was mad, they were both mad. They must know he was a person of importance, almost certainly a Member of Parliament. Now she seemed to be hinting that he was some scribbler, a mere novelist or something. It was too absurd; and very soon became absurder still, for suddenly the nurse, taking advantage of the doctor's seeming obliviousness and once again breaking all proper rules of nursing practice, sat on the edge of the bed.

'Look, Mr Green. Listen.' She bent her pretty capped head to read the top page, using a finger to trace the words, as she might have touched a new-born nose or tiny wrinkled lips. ' "It was conscious of a luminous and infinite haze, as if it were floating, godlike, alpha and o-me-ga ... " ' She flashed him a vivacious smile. 'Is that how you pronounce it, Mr Green? It's Greek, isn't it?' She did not wait for a reply, but went back to her reading. ' " ... over a sea of vapour and looking –" '

CRASH!

II

MNEMOSYNE, a daughter of Coelus and Terra,
mother of the nine Muses, by Jupiter, who
assumed the form of a shepherd to enjoy her
company; the word signifies *memory*. To
Mnemosyne is ascribed the art of reasoning
and giving suitable names to everything, so that
we can describe them, and converse about
them without seeing them.

       Lemprière, under *Mnemosyne*

ERATO, presided over lyric, tender and
amorous poetry; represented as crowned with
roses and myrtle, holding a lyre in her hand,
with a thoughtful, sometimes a gay and
animated look; invoked by lovers, especially in
April.

       Lemprière, under *Erato*

The door of the hospital room has been kicked open with savage violence. There stands an infinitely malevolent apparition straight out of nightmare; or more accurately, straight out of a punk rock festival ... black boots, black jeans, black leather jacket. Its gender is not immediately apparent; hermaphroditism appears most probable. The only certain thing is that it is in a towering rage. Beneath the black jacket, which is festooned with outsize safety-pins (another hangs from the left earlobe) and swastika badges, can be glimpsed a white T-shirt with a pointing pistol printed on it. The splintered shocks of hair above are also white, a staring albino white; whether by dye or bleach or in sheer horror at the face below, it is impossible to say.

The eyes are alarmingly haloed with kohl, giving an effect less cosmetic than as if their owner has recently been the loser in a fist-fight; and they match the mouth below, whose lips have seemingly been painted with the same black polish as that on the boots which have just kicked the door in. A left fist lies clenched on a hip, while the right hand grips the neck of an almost bodiless electric guitar. From it trails a short length of splay-ended flex, torn from the amplifier with such force that it has snapped in half.

But the ultimate horror is reserved for the last. Incredible though it may seem, there is, despite the hideous disguise, something familiar about the stance and facial bone-structure of the ghastly intruder. It is, after all, no hermaphrodite, but a she; and not any she, but the very twin of Dr Delfie on the bed. One can tell by the black-ringed eyes. One can also tell by the reaction of the target of this macabre clone's venomously accusing stare. Though evidently shocked, there are immediate signs that the would-be Member of Parliament is not entirely surprised. Pushing himself free with a speed and vigour markedly absent from his previous behaviour, he sits up on one arm and throws a frantic glance at his still procumbent partner; then back again at the gallows figure in the doorway; and finally speaks to it.

'You ...' he swallows. 'I ...' he swallows again.

The satanic double-ganger's only response to that is to march into the room and abruptly halt, legs astride. The neck of the guitar is thrust violently forward, as if it were a sub-machine gun, at poor defenceless Dr Delfie. A black-fingernailed hand rises and slashes down across the strings as a cut-throat razor might slash across a face in Glasgow. There is an indescribable clang of tortured arpeggio. A moment later there is no longer a Dr Delfie on the bed, only a faint depression where her head lay on the pillow.

Nurse Cory, who has sprung to her feet, opens her mouth to scream; but the merciless guitar is whipped to point at her, the steel strings are viciously slashed again. She too, pretty brown arms, blue-and-white uniform, astounded eyes, vanishes instantaneously into thin air, leaving nothing but a flutter of falling white typescript. Whang, wheeze, whang, goes the abominable guitar; into nothingness goes each sheet of paper.

Nemesis glares at the patient on the bed after this ruthless and lightning St Valentine's Day massacre, her eyes burning, still consumed by some maenadic fury. She less speaks than explodes.

'You *bastard*!'

Miles Green scrambles off the bed, hastily clutching at the rubber sheet and using it as an improvised apron.

'Now wait a minute. I think you have the wrong ward. And word.'

'You fuckin' chauvinist pig.'

'Steady on.'

'I'll give you steady on. Christ!'

'But you can't ... '

'I can't what?'

'Language like that.'

Her jet-black lips curl in a ferocious sneer. 'I can use any bleedin' language I bleedin' like. And I bleedin' well will.'

He retreats, holding the rubber sheet tight against his stomach.

'That gear. It isn't you at all.'

She takes a menacing step or two nearer.

'But we do just happen to know who I am.' The lips curl again. 'Despite the *gear*? Right?'

He would back further away, but realizes he is against the padded wall.

'It was just an idea.'

'Like hell it was. You lyin' sod.'

'A little try out. A first sketch.'

'My arse.'

'I thought I was never going to see you again.'

'Well you bleedin' well seein' me now. Right?'

He attempts to escape sideways, along the wall, but then finds himself at the corner, backed against the schoolgirls' breasts and faced with the threatening guitar-neck. She gives him a vitriolic stare, then suddenly stabs an outraged finger at his face.

'You realize what you done? You ruined my best bleedin'

53

gig in years. I had sixteen thousand kids screaming blue murder every time I hit a chord.'

'I can believe that.'

'You think I got nothin' better to do than piss around rubbin' out porn, you're out of your tiny mind.'

'I have a feeling we don't quite share the same register of discourse.'

She surveys him from head to foot, with a total contempt; but then her face twists into a mock grimace.

'Oh sure. I forgot. Plus the usual' – her mouth sags sarcastically sideways – 'deeper levels of meaning. Yuck.' She glowers, as if more than half inclined to spit in his face. 'You're pathetic. You don't even know where it's bleedin' at any more.'

'If you don't mind my mentioning it, I think you're rather overdoing "bleeding" in the stichomythia.'

'And you know where you can bleedin' well stick that!' She gives him another scorching look. 'Honest, you make me bloody vomit. Dr *A. Delfie.* That's not a pun, it's a dog's turd. And Nurse *Cory.* Gawd save us. Stinkin' elitist crap. I s'pose you think the whole soddin' world still speaks Greek.'

He throws her an oblique look, half dubious, half imploring.

'Don't say you've gone political.'

She shakes her head at him, in a new fury.

'Decent writin', i.e. non-bourgeois writin', was always political. 'Cept to middle-class zombies like you.'

'But you used to –'

'Don't you dare tell me what I used to. It's not my bleedin' fault if I was a victim of the historical male-fascist conspiracy.'

'But the last time we –'

'And don't give me that one!'

54

He looks down, then tries another tack.

'Lots of people would never have realized.'

'Screw lots of people.' She taps her thumb angrily back against the pistol on her T-shirt. 'You don't kid a sister. Not for one moment. All you are's a typical capitalist sexist parasite. You been nothin' but bad news, ever since I was stupid enough to give you the time of day.' He opens his mouth, but she jumps on. 'Tricks. Games. Always tryin' to have it both ways. But that's the last time you do it with me, you bugger.' She kicks backwards at the bed. 'Givin' that cardboard cut-out *my* face, *my* body.'

'It was only a very general description.'

'Bullshit.'

'We used to be such friends once.'

She mimics his voice. ' "We used to be such friends once." ' Her head shivers forward at him. 'I seen through you years ago. All you ever wanted out of me was a quick lay.'

'You're confusing me with Walter Scott. Or James Hogg, possibly.'

She closes her eyes, as if counting up to five; then her scathing eyes sear into his.

'God, if you was only a character too. If I could just rub you out along with your piddlin', pansy, paper, puppets.'

She wipes her mouth angrily with the back of her wrist. He leaves a little silence.

'You realize you're behaving just like a man?'

'And what's that s'posed to mean?'

'Instant value-judgements. Violent sexual prejudice. To say nothing of trying to hide behind the roles and language of a milieu to which you do not belong.'

'Oh belt up.'

'For a start you've completely confused the uniform of three quite different sub-cultures, to wit, the Skinheads, the

Hell's Angels and Punk. They're three rather different things, you know.'

'Will you shut up! Christ!'

Her eyes are like black fire again, but Miles Green senses that he has, at last, made a small counter-hit; for suddenly she turns away from him in his corner, lifts the strap of the guitar over her head and throws the instrument petulantly down on the end of the bed. For a moment she stands with her back to him. The rear of the black jacket is emblazoned with a white skull, under which are the words, in Nazi-Gothic capitals, DEATH LIVES. Then she turns, once more with an arm and finger out.

'Now just get this. From now on, I make the rules. Right? You ever again . . . *kaput*. End of gig. Is that clear?'

'As your native sunlight.'

She stares at him. 'Then get lost.' She folds her arms, and jerks her head sideways. 'Go on. Out.'

He raises the rubber sheet an inch or two.

'I've got nothing on.'

'Great. Now the whole friggin' world can see you for what you really are. And I hope you catch your death.'

He hesitates, shrugs, and takes a step or two over the old rose carpet towards the door; then stops.

'Couldn't we at least shake hands?'

'You're jokin'. You must be ravin' mad.'

'I do feel this is a bit of a verdict without a trial. I was simply trying to comment lightly on –'

She leans forward. 'Look. Ever since I got into serious liberation, you been takin' the mickey. I got your number, mate. You're the original pig. Numero Uno.' Her eyes flash at the door, and once again the skull-like head with its marionettish shocks of white hair jerks sideways. 'Out.'

He takes a further step or two, backwards now, like a courtier with ancient royalty, since the rubber sheet does not quite reach round his midriff, then once again stops.

'I could have made it far worse.'

'Oh yeah?'

'Had you swanning soppily through the olive-groves in a transparent nightie or something. Like Isadora Duncan on an off-day.'

Her hands go to her hips. Her voice becomes a hiss.

'Are you havin' the soddin' gall to suggest ... '

'I'm sure it had its points. In its time.'

She stands legs astride, arms akimbo. For the first time there is, beneath the anger, a glint of something else in her eyes.

'But it'd only make us giggle now, right? Is that it?'

He gives a modest shrug.

'It did always seem a touch absurd. Now you mention it.'

She nods at him, several times, then speaks between her teeth. 'Go on.'

'Not of course as a purely literary sort of concept. As part of the iconography of Renaissance humanism. Botticelli and all of that.'

'But cock?'

'I wouldn't dream of using such an ill-bred expression. Myself.'

She folds her arms again, and surveys him.

'Okay, let's have it – what would you use?'

'Daft? Wet? Slightly dotty?' He goes hastily on. 'I mean, heaven knows you can look terrific. That slinky little black number you wore last time we ... ' her arms drop, their fists clenched. He adds, rather weakly, 'Sensational.'

'Sensational?'

'Absolutely. I've never forgotten it.'

'And we all know what a great bleedin' judge you are.

57

Specially when it comes to degradin' women by turnin' us into one-dimensional sex-objects.'

'I think two would be –'

'Oh belt up.' She eyes him, then turns and picks up the guitar from the bed. 'You think you're so soddin' clever, don't you? "Iconography of the Renaissance" – Jesus. You don't know nothin' – you don't even know what I really looked like when I started. I've been through more bleedin' Renaissances than you've had toast for breakfast.'

'I realize.'

'Oh no you don't. You been askin' for this for years. And now you're bleedin' well goin' to get it. You smug bastard.'

Her right hand begins to pick a scale, a remote one, the Lydian mode. The transition is melting rather than instantaneous, yet extraordinary. The hair starts to soften and lengthen, to suffuse with colour; the hideous make-up drains from the face, the colour from the clothes; and the very clothes themselves begin to dissolve and modulate into a tunic of pure white samite. It leaves both arms and one shoulder bare and reaches to mid-calf. It is gathered at the waist by a saffron girdle. The material is not quite opaque where it is stretched. The boots vanish, she is barefoot. The now dark hair is bound up, in Grecian style. Round her forehead appears a small chaplet of pinkish-cream rosebuds among myrtle-leaves; and the guitar has become a nine-stringed lyre – on which, metamorphosis concluded, she now plays the same remote Lydian scale in reverse.

It is the same face, but it seems younger, as if she has lost five years; a honeyed golden warmth now in all the skin, enhanced by the clinging white fabric. And as for the overall effect: faces that launched a thousand ships are nothing. This one would make celestial motion itself stop, and look back. She lets the lyre fall; and lets him stare, open-mouthed, at unmistakable and immemorial divinity. But after a few moments her free hand rises to her hip. Some things, it seems, have not changed.

'Well ... Mr Green?'

Her voice has also lost its previous, and not entirely secure accent and intonation.

'I was totally wrong. You look stunning. Out of this world.' He seeks for words, or appears to do so. 'More childlike. Vulnerable. Sweet.'

'More feminine?'

'Incontestably.'

'Easier to exploit.'

'I didn't mean that at all. Honestly ... a dream. Just the sort of girl one would like to take home to meet mother. Even the rosebuds.'

Her voice is suddenly suspicious.

'What's wrong with my rosebuds?'

'They're from the hybrid tea Ophelia. I'm afraid it wasn't bred till 1923.'

'That's just typical. You're such a bloody pedant.'

'I'm sorry.'

'It happens to be my favourite rose. Since 1923.'

'And mine.'

She raises the lyre. 'And you can see an identical one to this, or what's left of it, in the Metropolitan Museum in New York. Before you start quibbling about that as well.'

'It looks undeniably authentic.'

'It *is* authentic!'

'Of course.'

She gives him a resentful look. 'And while you're about it, for goodness' sake stop staring at my breasts in that crudely obvious way.'

He stares at her bare, and exquisite, feet. 'Sorry again.'

'It's not my fault that the bra wasn't even invented then.'

'Absolutely not.'

'That monstrous chain upon true womanhood.'

'Hear hear.'

She contemplates him.

'I don't mind an occasional casual glance. That's another of your faults. You never leave anything at all to the imagination.'

'I will try.'

'Not here you won't. I've only done this to show you what you've missed. Not that you seem to appreciate it.' She turns away. 'If you must know most decent men fall to their knees when they first see me. As I really am.'

'I am on my knees. In spirit. You look ravishing.'

'By which all you mean is ravishable. You forget I know you through and through. And your miserable little monomaniac mind. All I'll ever be for you is just another bit of bird.'

'Not true.'

'Of course I don't expect you to compose hymns and odes and pour libations to me and' – she raises the lyre a fraction and lets it drop against her side – 'all that. When the world was still faintly civilized ... I'm perfectly well aware it's too much to expect from anyone in a crassly materialist age like this.' She throws him a half angry, half hurt look back over her bare shoulder. 'All I ask for is some minimal recognition of my metaphysical status *vis-à-vis* yours.'

'I'm sorry.'

'Well, you're too late.' She looks slightly upwards, as if addressing a very distant mountain-range. 'This last outrage is the final straw. I can overlook much, but not having my essential modesty of demeanour so grossly lampooned. Everyone knows my true nature is shy and retiring. I will not be turned into a brainless female body at your beck and call and every perverted whim. What you forgot is that I am *not* something in a book. I am supremely real.' She looks down at the carpet, and speaks in a lower voice. 'As well as being a goddess.'

'I've never denied it.'

'Oh yes you have. Every time you open your stupid mouth.' She puts the lyre down on the bed, and folds her arms, avoiding his eyes. 'I think I'd better warn you that I'm seriously thinking of bringing all this up at our next quarterly meeting. Because basically it's not just me who's being insulted, but my whole family. And frankly we've had enough. There's far too much of this about these days. It's high time someone was made an example of.'

'Truly sorry.'

She eyes him, then looks away again.

'You'll have to find a more convincing proof of it than that.' Now she raises her left forearm and glances at it, evidently forgetting, in a momentary absentmindedness, that like the rose Ophelia, the wrist-watch had not existed in classical times. She looks irritatedly round at the cuckoo-clock. 'I happen to have a very busy schedule today. I give you ten more sentences to make a full, proper and formal apology. This is your last chance. If I deem it acceptable, I am prepared to delay a decision over having you blacklisted. If not, you must take the consequences. In which case I should in all fairness strongly advise you to keep away from isolated trees and houses without lightning conductors for the rest of your life. Especially in stormy weather. Is that clear?'

'Yes, but it's not fair.'

She gives him a sharp glance. 'It is not only fair, but incredibly lenient in the circumstances. And now stop arguing.' She turns and picks up the lyre, then draws herself up slightly. 'You can start by getting on your knees. We can skip the kissing the traces of my footsteps bit, as I'm in a hurry. You have ten sentences. No more, no less. Then out.'

Holding his improvised apron firmly in position, he descends rather awkwardly to his knees on the carpet.

'Only ten?'

'You heard.'

She stares into the far corner of the room, waiting. He clears his throat.

'You've always been my perfect woman.'

She raises the lyre and plucks a string.

'Nine. And sickeningly trite.'

'Even though I've never understood you.'

Another pluck. 'You can say that again.'

'Completely.'

'Seven.'

'That's not a sentence. There wasn't a verb.'

'Seven.'

He stares at the sternly averted profile.

'Your eyes are like loquat pips, like Amphissa olives, like black truffles, like muscat grapes, like Chian figs ... hang on ... '

'Six.'

'I hadn't finished!'

She sniffs. 'You shouldn't have made such a meal of it.'

'There's never seriously been anyone but you.'

'Bloody liar. Five.'

'I can understand how you drive men mad.'

'Four. And women.'

He leaves a pause, searching her expression.

'Honestly?'

She gives him a quick glance down. 'I'm not going to be side-tracked.'

'Of course not. I just wondered.'

She addresses the wall. 'If you must know, that poor old bent teaspoon on Lesbos never got over seeing me undress one day for my morning swim.'

'Is that all that happened?'

'Of course it was all that happened.'

'But I thought –'

She throws him another impatient glance. 'Look, among the fifty thousand other things you've never realized about me is the fact that I wasn't born yesterday.' She looks away. 'Of course she tried all the usual dyke tricks. Wanted to photograph me in my bikini, and so on.'

'Photograph you in your . . .?'

She shrugs, quivers her head. 'Whatever it was then. Sculpt me or something. I can't remember every tiny detail. Now for heaven's sake get on with it. You've got three sentences left.'

'It was four.'

She breathes out. 'Very well then. Four. And they'd better be an improvement on the others.'

'The way you disappear, the way you return.'

She plucks the lyre twice. 'That's two.'

'That's ridiculous – it was clearly only a comma.'

'Not the way you said it.'

'It was just a pause for rhetorical effect. The concepts are linked. Disappearing, returning. Anyone can see that.' She gives him a warning look down. He says slowly, 'You really are the sexiest thing in all creation, you know that?'

She looks away. 'That's definitely two.'

'I can play by the rules as well, you know.'

'One.'

And she stands, with a hint of complacently superior inner knowledge, not very far from that characteristic of a famous type of Cycladic marble head, that is insufferable. He takes a deep breath.

'What I was actually rather wondering was this (colon) whether there aren't really (comma) in spite of your distinctly exaggerated umbrage at one or two small assumptions I was obliged to make in my fictional representation of you and for which you can in any case very largely blame your own extreme deviousness (bracket) if not positive coquettishness (dash) and I speak as one who has more times than he cares to remember been foully stood up by you without even the elementary courtesy of being warned that you were busy having it off with someone else (close bracket and comma) areas that merit further investigation by both the written and the writer (comma) or (comma) if you prefer (comma) between the personified as *histoire* and the personifier as *discours* (comma) or in simpler words still (comma) by you and me (semi-colon) and as I feel sure that we have at least one thing in common (colon) a mutual incomprehension of how your supremely real presence in the world of letters has failed to receive the attention (bracket) though you may regard that as a blessing in disguise (close bracket) of the campus faculty-factories (comma) the structuralists and deconstructivists (comma) the semiologists (comma) the Marxists (comma) academic Uncle Tom Cobleigh and all (comma) that it deserves (semi-colon) and furthermore as I'm sure a really thorough seminar *à deux* on the subject of ourselves will take time (comma) and I feel slightly at a disadvantage trying to cover my private parts with a rubber sheet (comma) while you (comma) on the other hand (bracket) though you do look absolutely delicious and truly divine with your pretty fingers poised like that over your wholly authentic lyre (close bracket and comma) do strike me as looking (dash) if it is not just a ghost of that frightful kohl (dash) the teeniest bit tired (comma) as well you might (comma) having sweetly come all this way (comma, or semi-colon if you prefer) then it occurred to me that we could do much worse than relax a little (dash) purely (comma) I hasten to add (comma) for the purposes of discussion (comma) of course (semi-colon) and I should add that the bed is exceptionally comfortable if you did feel like resting for a few minutes (dash) but I –'

'This is getting you absolutely nowhere!'

He smiles. 'I'm afraid I haven't quite finished.'

She stares at him, then turns and sits indignantly on the side of the bed, putting the lyre beside her. She folds her arms, and pointedly concentrates her gaze upon the cuckoo-clock.

'(Dot dot dot) to resume (dash) but I must insist that it is on the understanding that although I could go on like this forever (comma) until you would have to lie on the bed anyway out of sheer exhaustion (comma) we agree that the formal basis for our discussion must be your recognition of the indisputable fact that if you had only manifested yourself earlier in the text to which you object so much (dash) and especially in that stunning classical get-up (comma) or chiton (dash) the narrative development you most particularly take exception to would almost certainly not have taken place and we should therefore not be respectively standing and kneeling here in this absurd hospital room that I haven't even had the patience to describe properly by square old standards (comma) let alone *nouveau roman* ones (semi-colon) but (comma) and considering this is how I should have begun (comma) because you really are (dash) and I am not (underlined) being a male chauvinist (dash) one of the most god-awful cock-teasers in the history of this planet and I sometimes think how much easier the whole damn business would be if we were all gay and if you go on like this we very probably shall be and then where will you be (dash) back mooning around on that godforsaken mountain (comma) wailing those wretched chants in that uncouth Ionian dialect (comma) pinging away on that frightful lyre (dash) and while you're about it (comma) I wish you'd get the thing in tune (comma) the bass string's at least a semi-tone flat (comma) and do not let me forget that you'd be doing us all a great favour if you'd only ask your sister Euterpe or St Cecilia or actually just any moderately competent bouzouki player to give you a few elementary tips on how to hold a plectrum properly and –'

He has gone too far, at last. She snatches up the lyre and stands shaking it at him.

'If it wasn't such a performance getting these restrung, this would be framed over your moronic head. And don't you dare answer back! One single word and it ends *now*!'

It seems for a heart-stopping moment that she will fulfil her threat, despite the consequences. But she lets the lyre fall.

'In my entire four thousand years I've never met such arrogance. And the sheer blasphemy! I do *not* inspire pornography. I never have. And as for that other disgusting word ... everyone knows that my chief characteristic happens to be a supreme maidenliness – and once and for all will you *stop* looking at my nipples!' He hastily directs his eyes at the carpet again. She stares at him, then at her lyre, then at him again. 'I'm most terribly angry.' He nods. 'Immortally offended. Apart from anything else you seem to forget who I'm the daughter of.' He looks quickly up and shakes his head. She is not mollified. 'I can't help who he happens to be. I fall over myself to behave like one of you. Not to be a snob, not to go running to Daddy like some poor little rich girl.' She looks resentfully down at the carpet at her feet. 'And all you do is take advantage of my decency, my trying to keep up with the times.' She shows what is almost a pout. 'I'd just like to see you trying to be eternally young and several millennia old, all at the same time.'

Inasmuch as his muteness allows he tries to express the sincerest sympathy. She regards him for a long moment more, then suddenly turns and sits down again on the side of the bed, the lyre on her lap, and begins nervously tracing a decoration on one of its curved arms.

'All right. I may, heaven knows why, out of some misguided sense of responsibility, have inspired you with the mere gist of a notion of some new sort of meeting between us. But all I saw was an interesting little contemporary variation on an ancient theme. Something for learned readers. Not that obscene . . . ' she waves towards the head of the bed. 'I thought at least you'd have the sense to consult a few classical texts, for a start.' Her finger traces obsessively up and down the swan's neck of the golden-armed lyre. 'It's so unfair. I'm not a prig. And humiliating. If my wretched family gets to hear about it.' Her voice grows increasingly hurt. 'They think it's all a huge joke, anyway. Just because I thought I was clever drawing love poetry when we picked lots in the beginning. Then getting stuck with the whole of fiction as well. I have to work ten times as hard as all the rest of them put together.' She broods over her wrongs. 'Of course the whole genre is in a mess. Death of the novel, that's a laugh. I wish to all my famous relations it was. And good riddance.' She pauses again. 'It's what I loathe about this rotten country. And America, that's even worse. At least the French are doing their best to kill the whole stupid thing off for good.'

He gets to his feet. She sits with her head bowed; then throws the lyre to one side. After a moment she reaches for

67

her floral chaplet, pulls it off and starts sulkily fiddling with that instead.

'I don't know why I'm telling you all this. Fat lot you care.'

He cautiously advances, hesitates, then sits on the bed beside her, leaving the lyre between them. She gives the instrument a bitter side-glance.

'I know it's out of tune. I *hate* it. How the idea got around that the whole world fell silent when that ridiculous cousin of mine gave one of his endless concerts, God only knows. Tinkle, tinkle, plonk, plonk. Everyone I knew used to go to sleep with the sheer screaming boredom of it all.' She fiddles with the chaplet, as if it is to blame. 'And this absurd outfit. Don't think I don't know you're only pretending to like it.'

She flicks him a cold glance out of the corner of her dark eyes.

'Pig.' She tears at a rosebud. 'I hate you.' He waits. 'And you thought that black girl's boobs were much nicer, anyway.'

He shakes his head.

'I'm just amazed you didn't have her as well by the end. Or both of us together.' She pulls another rosebud out of the chaplet, and starts tearing its petals off, one by one. 'Properly developed, it could have been a perfectly tasteful and interesting idea. I'm not unreasonable. I wouldn't have objected to a certain discreet nuance of romantic interest. I'm not totally unaware that you're male and I'm female.'

He pushes the lyre back and edges a few inches closer.

'And don't think that's going to get you anywhere.'

He reaches and takes her hand; she tries to pull it free, but he insists. Their joined hands lie on the white sheet, prisoner and jailer. She gives them a contemptuous look, then away.

68

'Not if you got down on your knees again and begged me. And another thing. This is all strictly off the record.'

He squeezes the hand; then moves a little closer still, and after a further squeeze, puts his arm round her bare shoulders. She does not respond.

'I know exactly what you're trying to do. I may not be the musical one in my family, but I can recognize a fugal inversion when I see it.'

He bends and kisses the shoulder.

'I haven't the least liking or affection for you any more. It's just that I'm too tired to care. It was a bloody awful flight. I was air-sick.'

He kisses the shoulder again.

'You have absolutely no feeling for my feelings at all.'

He removes the rubber sheet. She throws a quick look down at his lap, then turns her head away.

'How unspeakably vulgar you are sometimes.'

He tries to lead her hand to the unspeakable vulgarity, but she snatches it away and folds her arms across her breasts again, staring at the quilted wall.

'You needn't think I didn't see that smirk on your face when I spoke of maidenliness. Just because once or twice in the past I may have allowed myself to relax in your presence. I suppose you think that's inconsistent and silly as well. That occasionally I have the humanity to contradict my own public image.'

He examines her profile, and then gently begins to ease the white strap of the tunic off her delectably rounded and golden shoulder. But she clamps her arm against her side when the whole top of the garment threatens to fall.

'And before you start thinking you're doing a marvellous seduction job, I'd better remind you that you're not the only one by a long chalk. I've had my clothes taken off by

69

sensitive geniuses. I'm not going to be impressed by a composer of erotica.'

He takes his hand away. There is a silence. Then, still staring at the wall, she slips the hanging strap under her elbow.

More silence. Still she stares at the wall.

'I didn't say you had to take your arm away.'

He puts it back.

'Not that I care a damn. Personally.'

He teases, very gingerly, the front of the tunic over what prevents it from falling to her lap.

'You think I know nothing about men. I can tell you my very first lover had more sex in his little toe-nail than you do in your whole boring body. Or he would have if he'd had a little toe-nail. You wouldn't have caught him just looking at the breasts of Miss Greece of 1982.' She adds, 'I refer to 1982 BC, of course.'

He raises his hand, and lets his other hand, around the shoulders, slip down to the bare waist and pull her a fraction closer. He leans to kiss her cheek; in vain. She turns her head away.

'But then he didn't have an infantile transferred fixation from golliwogs.' He clears his throat. 'I take that back. But then he didn't have an absolutely typical male pseudo-intellectual's sexist belief that making black sisters proves he's a liberal.'

There is a silence. She looks down at his right hand and its movements.

'I've a good mind to tell you about him. Just to put you in your place.' She watches a few moments more. 'And that happens to be a purely involuntary reaction. I can produce exactly the same effect using my own hands.' She sniffs. 'As I often have to, given how inept and ignorant most of you are.' His hand stops. She lets out an impatient breath. 'Oh

70

for God's sake. Now you've started, you may as well go on.' He goes on. 'I don't know why men put such enormous value on it. It's actually not half as exciting as you all so fondly imagine. It's only a biological survival mechanism. To facilitate suckling.' A moment or two later, with another sigh, she leans back, propped on her arms. 'Honestly. You're just like laboratory rats. The simplest trigger ... off you trot.' She subsides further, on her elbows. 'Nibble and bite. Bite and nibble.' There is a silence. But then she sits abruptly and pushes him away. 'You can't do that until you've undone my zone. Anyway, you're only trying to distract me. What you really need is a good bucket of cold water.' His hand is slapped. 'And stop that. It's a very complicated knot. If you want to do something useful for once, you'd better go and close the door. And turn the light out while you're about it.'

He goes to the door, and closes it on the impenetrable night that stands beyond. She is standing as well, by the bed, her bare back to him, her hands by her side, untying the saffron girdle. But just as she is about to slip the tunic down, she glances back at him over her shoulder.

'If you don't mind. We've already had quite enough voyeurism in this sickening room.'

He presses the switch at the door. The white panel above the bed is extinguished, but another panel above the door, apparently controlled from outside, continues to glow. It is dim, penumbral, like summer moonlight.

He opens his hands apologetically.

'Sod. You've just invented that.' He raises his hands in denial. 'Oh yes you have. There hasn't been a single mention of it before this.' She admonishes him with a long moment's accusing stare, then turns her back and steps out of the tunic. Now she faces him, holding the garment in front of her bosom, like some Victorian artist's model.

71

'You're really asking for it again. The only good line you came up with is when that doctor said you ought to be stuffed and put in a museum.'

She looks in the twilight for somewhere to hang her tunic; then walks round the end of the bed to the cuckoo-clock in the far corner. There she hangs it from a projecting chamois-head at the corner of one of the eaves. Without looking at him she returns to the bed, plumps up the pillows, and sits back in the centre of it with folded arms. He moves to join her.

'Oh no you don't. You can get the chair and sit there.' She points to a place on the carpet ten feet from the bed. 'And listen to someone else for once in your life.'

He fetches the chair and sits where she has indicated; then folds his arms as well. The Grecian-haired girl on the bed stares at him with an unconcealed suspicious resentment, then quickly at something lower down his body, before transferring her disdainful gaze to the light-panel over the door. There is a silence, during which his eyes do not leave her body. It is not a body, now it is revealed in all its beauty, that encourages leaving in any sense. It somehow contrives, all at the same time, to be both demure and provocative, classical and modern, individual and Eve-like, tender and unforgiving, present and past, real and dreamed, soft and ...

She gives him a fierce look. 'And for God's sake stop staring at me like a dog waiting for a bone.' He looks down. 'Unlike you I try to think before I tell a story.' He bows his head in assent. 'You'd better regard it as a tutorial. Not just about sexual arrogance, either. But on how to get simply and quickly to the point, instead of beating endlessly about the bush. Like some people I could mention.'

There is a further silence, then she begins to narrate.

'If you must know, it happened at home. I was only

72

sixteen. There was a place, a sort of alpine meadow sur-
rounded by dense undergrowth, where I used to go sometimes on my own to sunbathe. It was very hot, July, and I'd
taken off my tunic. A favourite aunt of mine – actually I've
always been more like a daughter to her than a niece – has
always held strong naturist views. It was she who first
taught me not to be ashamed of my body. Some people say
I look rather like her. She has a thing about sea-bathing as
well – summer and winter. But that wouldn't mean anything to you.'

She unfolds her arms and puts her hands behind her
head, still staring at the light over the door.

'Anyway. There I was in my meadow. A couple of nigh-
tingales singing in the bushes nearby. Wild flowers, buzzing
bees, all that sort of thing. The sun on my fifteen-year-old
back. Then I thought I might get burnt. So I knelt up and
rubbed some olive oil I'd brought all over my skin. I can't
imagine why, but as I was smoothing it in, instead of
reflecting on naturist principles I began thinking about a
young shepherd. By pure chance I'd met him once or twice.
His name was Mopsus. Purely by chance, on walks. There
was a beech-tree he used to loll about under when it was
hot. Playing a pipe, and if you think my lute is out of tune
... anyway. A month before my mother – you know about
my parents?'

He nods.

'She just had this thing about shepherds. After the di-
vorce.'

He nods again.

'Not that you could ever imagine, being a man. I mean
twins are bad enough. But nonuplets, and the whole lot
daughters. There had to be a limit, even in those days.' She
looks at him as if he might disagree; but he puts on his most
understanding face. 'I had to live with it all my childhood.

73

Constant rows over the alimony. I'm not entirely blaming Daddy, she went through more sets of lawyers than dresses at a sale. And anyway, heaven knows she made enough out of the nine of us once we were old enough. Talk about travelling freak shows. We were hardly ever off the road in the beginning. It was worse than being the Rolling Stones. And we had the most ghastly manager, our so-called musical uncle, he was an absolute pansy – of course that's why Mummy picked him, he had about as much interest in women as a film-star in anonymity. We used to call him Aunt Polly, Thalia and me. That's my only other sister who has a sense of humour. He used to pluck tweely away while we were supposed to prance around in our special costumes looking frightfully soulful and intelligent and all the rest of it. I mean that was the act. You've never seen anything so pathetic in all your life.'

He raises his eyebrows in gratitude for this valuable insight into primitive Greek religion.

'Apollo Musagetes, that was his real name. His stage name.'

Now his mouth opens, in some surprise.

'That's what irritated me so much when you talked of swanning through the olive-groves. Some chance. We'd hardly started menstruating before we were pushed off on our first tour. Pindus, Helicon, every wretched little mountain between. Honestly, I knew every temple dressing-room in Greece by the time I was fourteen. We might get booked in as the Glorious Muses. All we really were was the Delphi Dancing Girls. Most of it was about as much fun as playing Bradford on a wet Sunday night.'

He makes an appropriate gesture of prayer, for forgiveness.

'Pig. Anyway, my mother had this boy transferred off the mountain the month before. Two of my sisters had complained about something they'd seen him doing, I was never told quite what. Apparently he was being rather beastly to one of his ewes. That was it, of course. Out he went. I can't imagine why he should have crossed my mind that particular day.'

She reclines a little further back, and raises her knees; then extends one leg in the air, turning and inspecting the slim ankle for a moment, before bringing it back to its partner.

'Actually . . . oh well, there was something, I suppose I'd better tell you. Again, by pure chance, one day before he was given the boot, I was walking on my own and happened to pass near his beech-tree. It was terribly hot that day, too. I was rather surprised to notice he wasn't there, though all his smelly old sheep were. Then I remembered, Olympus knows why, that there was a spring not far away. It came out of a cave and made a little pool. Actually it was our pool, it was supposed to be a kind of combined bath and bidet for my sisters and myself, but never mind. Anyway, I had nothing better to do, all this was in that absolutely marvellous time before the alphabet and writing was invented – my Zeus, if we'd only realized. We should be so lucky.' She throws him a dark look. 'So I went to the pool. He was having a bathe. Naturally I didn't want to disturb his privacy, so I slipped behind some bushes.' She glances at the man on the chair. 'Is this boring you?'

He shakes his head.

'You're quite sure?'

He nods.

'I was only fourteen.'

He nods again. She turns on her side, towards him, and curls up her legs a little. Her right hand smooths the sheet.

'He came out of the Pierian Fountain – that was Aunt Polly's prissy name for this pool – and sat on a rock beside it to dry. And then – he was only a simple country boy, of course. Actually, to cut a long story short, he began ... well, playing with a rather different sort of pipe. Or syrinx, as we called it. He obviously thought he was alone. I was frankly quite shocked. Disgusted. It wasn't that I hadn't seen naked men before, at my aunt's in Cyprus.' She looks up. 'Did I tell you she lived in Cyprus?'

He shakes his head. She goes back to smoothing the sheet.

'Anyway. As a matter of fact I'd always thought their little hanging things looked rather silly. All that horrible pelt surrounding them. I couldn't understand why they shaved their beards every day, but not that. Why they couldn't see that my aunt and her women friends and I looked so much prettier.' She looks up again. 'I suppose you did notice?'

He smiles and nods.

'She hates anything that spoils natural line. On purely aesthetic grounds.'

He opens his hands.

'I suppose you think it's just one more freakish thing about me.'

He denies it, but there is this time a faint hint of a shrug as well; of a secret doubt conquered by a polite refusal to argue. She eyes his bland expression, then sits up on an arm.

'It's a sculpturesque thing. My aunt has all sorts of brilliant artist friends. They all agree.' He opens his hands. 'And it's not just the visual side. It's the plastic aspect as well.' He nods. She scrutinizes him. 'You do think it's freakish, don't you?' He gives her a slightly embarrassed smile, and looks down. She watches him a moment or two more, with a slight frown, then pushes herself up and kneels erect on the bed, facing where he sits, her thighs tightly

76

pressed together. 'Look, I haven't forgiven you one bit, and don't get any ideas, but because this is a tutorial and you don't seem to understand the point I'm making, I give you permission for one quick assessment of . . . that latter aspect.' Her hands reach down and trace two lines. 'As a matter of fact these are called after my aunt. Aphrodite's dimples.' She looks up. 'That was her name.'

He nods. Now she puts her hands behind her back, staring at the wall beyond him, like a schoolgirl waiting to be awarded a prize. He rises and goes to the bed and sits on its edge beside her; then brushes the tips of his fingers across the plastic aspect.

'I do it with a special depilatory. It's herbal. A little man at Ktima. Near my aunt's home.'

A silence. Then her hands suddenly come round and give him a sharp push away.

'I was asking you to appreciate *external* form. From a purely artistic standpoint. You're worse than a child. It's absolutely impossible to have a serious conversation with you.' She turns and sits back as she had originally, with her arms folded, back against the pillows. 'Pig.' She kicks sideways with her left foot. 'Oh sit there. If you must. But keep your hands to yourself.' He stays on the edge of the bed; bends; then straightens, looks into her dark eyes.

'Pervert.'

He moves a fraction closer up the side of the bed.

'One can't give you a single inch.' He leans an arm across her waist. She raises a hand to keep him firmly at that distance. 'Just because I haven't got any clothes on, it doesn't mean you have to behave like a Neanderthaler. The analogy I was trying to suggest was the classical symposium. You've just invented a completely non-existent light-panel. Why on earth you can't make a second bed or an Attic day-couch as well, I simply don't know.'

He smiles. She smoulders.

'I know men who'd give their right arm to hear this very personal chapter from my autobiography. Why I should pick you of all people ... I've a jolly good mind to stop.' He waits. 'And I would if I didn't know you'd go around saying I chickened when it came to it. You'd just love that.' She looks past him. 'Anyway, you're not going to get out of hearing it now.'

She folds her arms a little tighter still; then, avoiding his eyes, goes on.

'I now know that by pure chance my visual initiation was being conducted by an exceptionally well-endowed young male. In some peculiar way I found my disgust changing to a sort of pity for him. He was rather like you. Such a flagrant narcissist that one couldn't really apply ordinary standards. It's always been my weakness. I'm much too softhearted with mental cripples. Anyway. In the end I wanted to go and ask him to be gentler with himself. He seemed to be doing such peculiar, brutal things. I thought he was angry with it or something. Of course I didn't, I was too shy. I was only thirteen. I slipped away in the end, I tried to pretend it had never happened. But I've always had rather a vivid imagination. Been retentive of images.'

She breaks off. 'You're not even listening.'

He looks up and nods.

'If you think that gives me the least ... oh I don't know, I give up.' She raises her right knee. 'I suppose children ... go on. Thirty seconds' free period.' Her hands go back behind her head again, and tilting it back resignedly on the top pillow, she stares at the ceiling, then closes her eyes. Near the end of the thirty seconds, taking advantage of her shut eyes, he kisses along the beautiful young Greek body to a throat whose only rival is Nefertiti's; but when he bends for the mouth her hands catch his shoulders and push him back again.

'*No.*'

He stays leaning over her. She sinks a little deeper into the pillows, as if trying to escape from him, and stares sombrely up at his face.

'You're not going to stop me finishing, so don't think you are.'

He nods.

'If by some miracle you can get your mind off that eternal one track it runs along, perhaps you'll remember that all this began in my meadow.' He nods. 'To be perfectly frank, when I'd finished oiling myself I lay on my tummy, in the innocent way schoolgirls do.' Her eyes survey his. 'If you can picture that. How defenceless I was, how exposed.' He looks slightly aside, frowns. 'Oh God, you're impossible. You're like all your age. Words are just grey porridge to you. Nothing's real until you see it on television.' He shrugs, a victim of fate and history. She hesitates, lets out a breath, then twists round on her stomach, with her head turned sideways on the pillow. 'Perhaps you can get some dim idea of the scene now. As a matter of fact this wasn't quite all. By an extremely unfortunate chance a little tussock of grass was pressing into me and I was trying to rub it flat with motions of my hips. I realize now I was unconsciously laying myself open to misinterpretation.'

There is a silence, broken only by another sigh of impatience from the narratress. She continues.

'They're such cunning brutes, he must have crept up in the undergrowth. And there's something even worse about them, they're telepathic, they can read minds. It's something to do with their animal half. So he not only saw what I was doing, he must have also known what I was thinking. Then, at a most ... embarrassing moment, just as the

79

imaginary young shepherd was doing something to me I'm too modest to specify, and which of course I would never have dreamed of allowing in reality – to my horror I felt the intruder's hairy body and . . . something else lower itself on my innocent twelve-year-old olive-oiled bottom.' There is a silence. 'Oh honestly. Do you have *always* to be so literal-minded?'

He kisses the nape of her neck.

'I wanted to scream, to struggle. But I knew it would be in vain. It was either surrender to his lust or be murdered. Actually he wasn't violent at all. He did bite my neck, but only in play. Then started to whisper things. Wicked things, but I forced myself to listen. Things about other women, other girls – even, I was amazed to hear, about the very one of my sisters, my eldest, who'd made the most fuss about the shepherd-boy. She's actually the most incredible hypocrite. If historians only . . . but never mind.' She pauses a moment. 'As a matter of fact after a bit he didn't feel quite so awful as I'd expected. He had lovely brown skin, and the furry part of his body was much nicer than you might think. Not coarse at all. Like mohair. Or angora.' She pauses another moment. 'Nor did he squash me to death.' Her listener raises himself a little. She twists her head and gives him a mistrustful glance back up out of the corner of her eyes. 'Nor did he do what's running through your over-active mind. Actually he had the decency to turn me round.' A few moments later she resumes, staring up into his eyes. 'I was beyond resisting by then. Mere wax in his hands. I could only stare up into his lascivious, lecherous eyes. If you can imagine that.'

He smiles down into her dark ones, and nods.

'It's not funny.'

He shakes his head.

'He made me open my legs . . . I did fight a little then,

but he was too strong, too excited.' She closes her eyes. 'I can still feel it.' Again she is silent for a few moments, then opens her eyes again on his. Her ankles cross and lock themselves together on top of his legs. 'It was ghastly: unadulterated biological domination. My tender eleven-year-old mind hated every moment of it. Every brutal inch of this abominable violation. I decided I would never forgive him. Or his sex. That from then on for the rest of my life it must be war, war to the hilt against all male things. I would torture and torment every man who crossed my path. Oh I might let them believe I enjoyed their caresses, their kisses, their fondling hands. But deep down I remained, even as I was being deflowered, the eternal virgin.' She gives him a solemn look. 'I forbid you ever, ever to tell a soul about this.'

He shakes his head: never.

'I did once tell someone else. Like a fool.'

He conveys surprise.

'Of course he had to blab it all out at the next opportunity. And from the usual male-chauvinist angle. When it was so obviously *my* story. I may be a lot of things, but I'm not just an idiot pair of nymphs in some fancy Frog poet's afternoon off.' She adds, 'Present company, please note. And if you're wondering why he made me into two, he was blind drunk. As usual. His name was Verlaine.'

He shakes his head quickly.

'Or something. One of that lot.'

He tries to mouth the correct syllables. She contemplates him.

'Your arms ache? Well you should jolly well have thought of that before you had that ridiculous doctor in the same posture. You're like all pornographers. As soon as it's a question of his lordship's pleasure, reality flies out of the window.' She looks at his lips, then into his eyes again.

'Honestly, I begin to find you almost more unpleasant dumb than talking. You can speak again now. If you absolutely must.' But she goes on before he can open his mouth. 'And as long as you don't think the carnal side of this conversation has any bearing on my real opinion of you. Or on my metaphorical disgust for all you and your sex stand for. And don't think I haven't seen through your painfully obvious manoeuvrings to get me into this position.' The legs behind his lock a little more firmly, and she sinks slightly lower. 'I'm not enjoying it one bit. And I don't suppose you are. I'm sure you'd much rather be having some boring discussion about the parameters of contemporary narrative structure.'

'Have a heart. Actually, my arms *are* killing me.'

'You can get on your elbows. But no more.'

He lies with his face just above hers.

'I want to kiss you.'

'Well you can wait. I haven't finished about what happened on the mountain yet. Now I've forgotten where I was.'

'Being deflowered one afternoon. By a faun.'

'They're not like ordinary men. They're tetrorchid, if you must know. They can do it again and again. And he did.'

'Always the same way?'

'Of course not. We went through the whole alphabet.'

'But you've just said it wasn't –'

'If it *had* been invented.'

'Twenty-six times?'

'Wake up. We're in Greece.'

'Twenty-four?'

'Plus several diphthongs.'

'Them I can't quite see. In context.'

'And you're not going to. The point is this. For all my

outrage and anger and the rest of it I had to admit he was a superb lover. Superbly imaginative. The exact opposite of you, in fact.'

'That's not fair.'

'You're not in a position to know. I thought each time would have to be the last. But each time he'd find some new way of exciting me. He made me want to be like him, a wild animal. It went on for hours and hours ... and hours. I lost all sense of time. From sigma onwards I could hardly do anything, I was so exhausted. But I didn't mind. I'd have been happy to go back to alpha again. With him.'

She falls silent.

'That's it?'

'You haven't been listening at all.'

'I have.'

'You wouldn't just say "that's it" in that odiously amused way, if you had. You'd be apologizing for ever having had the nerve to suppose your own puny imagination could equal a real-life event such as that.'

He reaches a finger and traces the outline of her lips.

'You must have been a phenomenal eleven-year-old virgin.'

'I hadn't finished up all the olive oil. If you must know.'

He taps her nose. 'That's a flagrant pinch from the *Carmina Priapea*.'

'My own unique and shatteringly sensual experience happens to predate that stalely obscene collection by at least two thousand years.'

'I'll believe the lying on your stomach.'

She leaves a silence; and the more he smiles the more she, so to speak, unsmiles.

'Are you trying to imply I made the rest of it up?'

He amusedly taps the nose again. 'You know as well as I do that satyrs were always pure myth.'

There is a minute contraction of her eyes, and even what seems a darkening of the already dark irises.

'Oh yes?'

Still he smiles. 'Yes.'

'You're hurting my breasts.'

With a sigh he pushes himself off her body again. Behind him he feels her legs unlock. Then she folds her arms and stares up at him. It is as if a cloud has passed over her, an abrupt phasal change taken place. And still he smiles.

'I adore it when you pretend to be angry.'

'I *am* angry.'

'Come on. A joke's a joke.'

'Are you saying you don't believe a word I've said? Is that it?'

'We've talked enough.'

'I want an answer.'

'Come on.'

'I wish you'd stop using that stupid cliché.' Her face is totally without humour. 'Do you or do you not believe what I've just told you?'

'Metaphorically.'

She stares coldly up at him. 'This is the way you want it now, is it?'

He no longer smiles. 'I haven't the least idea what you're talking about.'

'The unvarnished truth, yes?'

'You know perfectly well why you were landed with fiction. It was nothing to do with picking the short straw. It's just that you could always lie ten times better than all the rest of your sisters put together.'

'What sisters? I haven't got any sisters.'

'Oh sure. Your name isn't Erato and –'

'No my name is *not* Erato! And you're absolutely right. Of *course* satyrs are pure myth. Of *course* that grotesque

84

scene never took place. Especially as it involved not one, but *two* entirely mythical beings.'

He stares down at her; she stares fiercely back.

'And what is that supposed to mean?'

'I'm calling your disgusting, prototypal male bluff, that's what it means. And I'll tell you what a modern satyr is. He's someone who invents a woman on paper so that he can force her to say and do things no real woman in her right mind ever would.'

'I don't know what you're trying to –'

'I've fallen over myself to behave as you want so far. As well as I can without being physically sick. And all the reward I get is to be made fun of at the end of it.'

'Erato!'

'Don't be ridiculous. I can't be Erato. She never existed. And even if she had if you think she'd have come within ten light-years of this hideous room, let alone taken her clothes off and let you . . . honestly. Grow up.'

'Then who the devil do you think you are?'

'I don't think, I know. I'm just one more miserable fantasy figure your diseased mind is trying to conjure up out of nothing.' She turns her head to one side. 'I wish to God you'd just bang away and get it over with. Then throw me on your next bonfire.'

He stares down at the profiled face on the pillow.

'Fantasy figures aren't allowed wishes. I shall take as long as I like. Correction. As I fucking well like.'

'I thought your type died out with the Ottoman Empire.'

'Or even longer. As you aren't real.'

She looks angrily up at him again.

'I only seem real because it is your nauseating notion that the actually totally unreal character I'm supposed to be impersonating should do so. In fact a real me in this situation would avoid all reference to the matter, especially as she would never have got herself into the situation in the first place. If she had any choice. Which she doesn't. As she isn't real.' She cranes and shivers her head at him. 'You're doing exactly what you always do: chasing your own tale.'

'Very funny. And how do you know what I always do?'

'I don't.'

'But you've just –'

She turned her head sideways. 'All I do is parrot whatever lines you give me. They're yours. Not mine.'

'Balls.' She remains disgustedly turned away. 'You're just my words? Mere wax in my hands?'

'I should have thought cheap plasticine was more accurate.'

He takes a breath. 'Without a whisper of volition of your own?'

'I'd have left this room hours ago if I had.'

'I could do anything to you, and you'd just lie there?'

'No such luck.' She sniffs. 'Knowing the putrid harem of your imagination, you'd have me squirming about and egging you on.'

He pounces. 'How do you know my imagination?'

'"Know" is an epistemological nonsense, in the circumstances.'

'Never mind. You used it.'

'Because it's so crudely repetitive one has to be its victim for only a few pages to guess how it will always work.'

'And how on earth can a harem be putrid?'

'You should try living in one. Instead of just owning it.'

He stares down at her. 'I'm not putting a single word of this into your mouth.'

'I wouldn't be caught dead in your dialogue. Of my own free will. If I had one.'

'If you ask me, you're talking exactly as you want. I.e.,

as a perverse little bitch who's about as straightforward as a right-angle bend and as chaste as a go-go dancer.'

'Thank you.'

'I'm not fooled for a moment. This is just the sort of situation you love. Turn up, then be wilfully obstructive from the first word on. And what's more, you know it. Don't you?'

'If you say so. That is, if you say "if you say so" is what you want me to say. As it apparently is.'

'I demand a proper answer.'

'At last he speaks naturally.'

'I consider I have a right to a proper answer.'

'Then you'd better think of one.'

'It certainly wasn't *that*.'

She shrugs. 'Then try again. You're the master.'

He angrily contemplates her averted face. There is a silence, then he speaks.

'I've just caught you.'

'How?'

'By telling you to do something. Which you haven't.'

'I'm not a mind-reader. Merely your inflatable doll.'

'Very well. I want the inflatable doll to tell me she loves me. Passionately. At once.'

'I love you. Passionately.'

'Not like that. With feeling. *Con amore*.'

'I don't see how I can.'

'Well well well.'

She looks contemptuously up at him.

'It's not my fault that I'm equally the programmed slave of whatever stupid mood you've created. Whatever clumsy set of supposed female emotions you've bodged up for me. To say nothing of *your* character. I notice there's not been a single word about his exceedingly dubious status. I wonder who's pulling *his* strings?'

'I am. I'm me. Don't be ridiculous.'

She gives him a sarcastic little smile, and looks away. 'God you're so naïve.'

'You're the one who's naïve. I woudn't tell my own character to suggest I'm not really me.'

'Then why's he being referred to as "he" throughout? What are you trying to hide?'

He is silent a moment.

'Look, I'm not going to pursue this totally irrelevant red herring. You're only trying to get out of explaining why you won't do what I ask.'

'I could probably simulate it physically. Start clutching and moaning. Would that do?'

'It would not.'

'Then I suggest your character tries it. You make *him* tell me he loves me passionately.' She turns her head sideways again on the pillow. 'I'm waiting.'

'I know your trouble. You're a classic spoilsport. As soon as you start enjoying it, you feel guilty. Sidle off into all this crap about reality and unreality.'

'I shouldn't start talking about that, if I were you.'

'Meaning?'

'My God, when I think in this day and age ... it's pathetic. The world's full of highly pertinent male-female situations whose fictional exploration does subtend a viable sociological function – and yet this is the best you can come up with. Muses ... I mean, Christ. It's so embarrassing. As if any contemporary woman who actually existed would talk in that revoltingly fey, coy way about shepherds and pipes and –'

'Women who talk about explorations that subtend viable sociological functions are just as bad.'

'Oh, I know it's very wicked of us. To show we can actually think. Whatever next.'

'You are viciously and sadistically breaking all the rules.'

Her face flares round. 'Your rules!'

'All right. My rules.'

She looks away again. 'I'm sick to death of them. Of having to pretend I exist in a way I never would, if I did.'

'You damn well exist for me, anyway. Just as you are.'

'Heil Hitler.'

'Okay. For the sake of argument: Hitler says you exist. As you are.'

'He can't. You have to have certain elementary freedoms to exist.'

'If you must know, if there was anyone here, they'd think you were real enough by now. And a bloody sight too real.'

'And if you must know, I think you're the most maladroit, unpleasant and dishonest man I've ever been to bed with.'

'That's a perfect example of your asinine female logic! First you don't exist. Then you've been endlessly screwed by other men. Come on, make up your mind – which is it, for heaven's sake?'

'I am perfectly capable of making the kind of comparison I might have made, had I existed as I actually am. If I was.'

'You can't not exist and actually be. They're mutually contradictory.'

'I see. Now I'm denied even an imagination.'

'Oh God. I give up.'

'I'm not even allowed to think of what I might have been if I hadn't had the misfortune to be created by you. Not allowed to think of all the sympathetic, intelligent, fastidious artists who might have invented me first. Instead I have to pick the one rotten apple, the one born bungler, the one bull in a china-shop who couldn't appreciate my delicacy and subtlety of mind in a billion years.'

'You ungrateful . . . you'd be nothing without me!'

'I wish to God I was. I'm worse than nothing with you.' She stares contemptuously up at him. 'The honest and simple truth is that you don't begin to understand my potential.' She turns her head away. 'It's not really your fault, I suppose. Given your technical hamhandedness, I don't see how you ever could.'

'What do you mean by that? What hamhandedness?'

'It's obviously escaped your notice, but it wouldn't have escaped that of any unfortunate third party forced to be a witness to all this, that we remain in quite ludicrously inappropriate sexual congress together.'

'That's soon remedied.'

He pulls abruptly back and stands off the bed; returns to the chair, sits on it and crosses his arms, then his legs. He stares studiously across the room at the wall. She gives him a pent look, then props herself up on an elbow and turns her back on him. There is a silence. At last she speaks in a small, flat voice.

'If it's not asking too much, I wonder if you'd mind inventing something practical for once. Like some clothes for me. Then I could put them on and leave. Anything will do. Just a dressing-gown.'

'I have something to say first.'

'Everything's been said. *Ad nauseam*.'

'Oh no it hasn't.' The naked young woman gives a silent sigh and puts her clenched left hand on her hip, the elbow cocked, in a gesture of resignation under duress. He stares at her back, then speaks in a quieter voice. 'I will concede that I have made one grave error. Not about you, but about her. All right, perhaps she doesn't exist in a historical or scientific sense. But as you're so subtle-minded I'm sure you'll agree that she has acquired a kind of apostrophic and prosopopoeic reality.'

90

'Do get on with it. And I wish you'd try to stop talking like a dictionary.'

He draws a breath. 'But as she doesn't exist, and we both now agree that you aren't her, I can speak frankly. My mistake was embodying, if she did exist, a totally immoral and persistent old tart like that in an at least outwardly quite attractive girl like you. I mean what would she really be by now – if she had existed? She's been a hot night out for every pen-pushing Tom, Dick and Harry, a pair of ever-open legs, for four thousand years. I ought to have made her a raddled old syphilitic hag. At least that might have been within spitting distance of the truth. Don't you agree?'

'Are we finished?'

'Moreover, she ought – if she did exist – to do a little market research on herself. Try knocking on a few doors. "Hi. My name's Erato. I sell inspiration on the never-never. Can I interest you in an epithalamion? May I show you our new bargain line in personalized alcaics?" They'd just laugh in her face. If they didn't think she'd escaped from the nearest nuthouse.' He eyes the turned back. 'Anyway, they can do all she used to do by computer and word-processor now, and fifty times better. I could even feel faintly sorry for her, poor old milked-out cow. If she did exist.'

Now it is the girl on the bed who takes the deep breath. But she remains silently staring away into the corner of the room.

'I've only to look at you lying there, in that Rokesby Venus pose, to see how ridiculous it was. Obviously by now she'd be some old biddy bundled in an overcoat fishing round dustbins and muttering . . . if she did exist.'

This somewhat abrupt ending (or aposiopesis) is caused by a previous movement from the figure on the bed. At the mention of the Rokesby Venus, she has turned and sat up. Now, her arms folded, she regards the man on the chair with tight-pressed mouth and eyes gone as hard as obsidian.

'Have you quite finished now?'

'Yes.'

'I bet she wishes she was a raddled old hag. Then at least she could retire. Somewhere where men don't exist.'

'But it scarcely matters, does it? As she doesn't, either.'

'I'm simply speaking on your own assumption.'

'Which is laughably hypothetical.'

'And typically chauvinist.'

He tilts his head and examines the cocked toes of his crossed leg. 'I'm surprised you should say that.'

'That I take my own sex's side?'

'Just that if she did exist, yet wasn't here, it would have to mean she was leaving all the dirty work to you. It's your body that has to undergo the vile sexual humiliation of having to please mine. Which makes her no better than a procuress. No?'

'I notice you're very characteristically leaving out of account her whole historical situation.'

'I'm not sure I like this purely theoretical element you're introducing.'

'Unlike you, I happen to have considerable powers of empathy. I am merely putting myself in her existential place.'

'If it existed.' She raises her eyes to the ceiling. 'Just as long as we're both clear we are conducting a completely abstract and unreal disputation. Essentially in the same category as the old scholastic one about the number of angels who can play hopscotch on a needle's point.' He opens his hands. 'The floor is yours.'

She stares at him. 'I suppose it's never occurred to you what a horror it would be, if it existed, to have to occupy a role and function that escapes all normal biological laws. All on her own. No outside help, never a day off. Constantly having to dress up as this, dress up as that. The impossible boredom of it. The monotony. The schizophrenia. Day after day of being mauled about in people's minds, misunderstood, travestied, degraded. And never a word of thanks for it. Never –'

'Wait a minute. What about –'

Her voice rises. 'Never a thought for her as a person, only for what can be got out of her. Never a moment's consideration for her emotions. Never enough imagination to realize that she may be secretly dying for a little tenderness and sympathy, that she's also a woman and can't help it if certain combinations of circumstances and mood do make her need the services of a male body in an entirely *natural* female way – which has absolutely nothing to do with humiliation, by the way, and . . .' she takes a breath. 'But what's that matter if his lordship, whoever he is, wants something else. If he wants to play *his* games, leaving her –'

'I did not start this.'

'Screaming with frustration.' She looks away at the wall. 'If she existed, of course.'

He contemplates his cocked foot again.

'This dressing-gown – is there any particular colour or material you'd like?'

'I hate you.'

'How about green then?'

'You'd just love that, wouldn't you? She has the effrontery to object to being treated as a mere sex-object, so out with her. Toss her back to nothingness, like an old boot.'

'You asked for it yourself, only a minute ago.'

She stares furiously at him for a moment, then once more

twists abruptly on her side, her back to him, facing the far wall.

'I'm not going to say another word. You're impossible.' There is silence for five seconds. 'You're like all men. Once that absurd bit of dangling tissue between your legs has had its fun, all you think of is how fast you can get rid of us.'

'I'd have got rid of you long before now, if that was true. You've just convinced me I can do what I like.'

'Exactly!'

'Exactly what?'

'I have absolutely no rights. The sexual exploitation's nothing beside the ontological one. You can kill me off in five lines if you want to. Throw me in the wastepaper basket, never think of me again.'

'I don't think there's much chance of that.'

'Oh yes you would. Just like all the others.'

'What others!'

'Oh don't be so absurd.' She darts a contemptuous look back over her shoulder at him. 'Are you trying to suggest I'm the first?'

'It's . . . possible you're not the first.'

'And possible I shan't be the last?'

'It's possible.'

'So it's more than *possible* that I'm just the latest of a series of wretched imaginary women who've had the misfortune to fall into your hands. To be kicked out the moment someone more attractive walks past.'

'As a matter of record my relationship with them was and continues to be deeply human and rewarding on both sides. In every case we remain excellent friends.'

'They sound like a first-class bunch of female Uncle Toms to me.'

'I'm not going to reply to language like that.'

'Surprise, surprise.'

'Only the other day one of them told me she thought I'd given her far too much freedom in our liaison.'

'Before you killed her off.'

'I do not kill my female friends off.'

'Much. You just collect and mummify them. Lock them up in a cellar and gloat over them, like Bluebeard.'

'I find that a singularly offensive comparison.'

'For a plurally offensive habit. Otherwise known as necrophilia.'

He stands up.

'All right. That's it. You've just said you'd rather be nothing without me than worse than nothing with me. So okay. Your choice. There's the door.' He flicks his thumb at it. 'There. Now there's a green bathrobe on it. Simple. You stand off the bed, you walk to the door, you put on the robe, you leave, we forget the whole thing. It never happened. Your move.'

She casts a look towards the door, then once more turns away. There is a silence. She draws up her legs a little, turns away a fraction more.

'I'm cold.'

He goes and fetches the green bathrobe; returns to the bed and drapes it roughly over her shoulders. Then he sits down again on the chair. She says nothing, but then, with a curious slowness, as if she hopes he may not notice, she lets her body sag and her face sink down into the pillow. The silence grows. Her left hand moves surreptitiously up from under the bathrobe and touches her eyes. There is a faint, stifled outbreath. He stands and goes to the bed again, half extends a hand towards her shoulder, but then changes his mind. Another stifled outbreath. He sits on the side of the bed, his back to her, untouching; but speaks more neutrally.

'We're not being very consistent.'

Her voice is almost a whisper, on the brink of breaking.

'It's because you'll never admit you're wrong about anything. You're so unkind to me. You don't know how alone I feel.'

'We were both enjoying it. Until you –'

'I can't enjoy it when I have no status at all. When I don't even know who I'm really supposed to be. When I know it may end at any moment.'

'I had no intention of ending it.'

'Well how was I to know?'

'It was perfectly jolly teasing.'

'No it wasn't. You were needling me all the time. Just taking advantage of my helplessness.'

'Now you're being paranoiac.'

'I'm *not*.' He feels her shift, and glances round. She is looking at him over the bathrobe, her eyes still wet; and personifying every hurt and helpless female face, caught between reproach and appeal for sympathy, since time began. 'I didn't even exist at all a few hours ago. I'm as innocent as a new-born baby. You *don't* realize.'

It is a face even more beautiful and seductive in tears than in its other states. He turns rather sharply away.

'I didn't start it.'

'But you did. You gave me that whole impossible spiel about the satyr to deliver and then promptly told me I was lying. That I'm as chaste as a go-go dancer. You know, it's like being a ponce, then accusing one of your girls of being a whore.'

'I take the expression back. Consider it erased.'

'I suddenly felt, what am I doing here letting this total stranger humiliate and insult me like this – distort what I really am. I mean I know I'm technically nothing. But what I begin to feel I would be if I wasn't. My true, serious nature.'

'I've already admitted I'm wrong about her. Erato.'

'I don't care about her. I care about *me*.'

'All right.'

'I'm not like that. I know I'm not.'

'I've said all right.'

'It was so crude. So blatant.'

'I'm prepared to admit that making you so incredibly beautiful was a mistake on my part.'

'You don't begin to understand what women like me are about.'

'I realize I should have given you a heavy chin, fat legs, a squint, acne, bad breath ... I don't know. Whatever would have given your true serious nature a chance to shine through.'

There is a silence.

'It's too late for that now.'

'I don't see why. I was just thinking. I've already changed your appearance twice. Full consultation this time, of course. You could tell me the specific ways in which you'd like to be totally unattractive to men.'

'You only changed my clothes. Not my basic body. It would seem absurd.'

'I could always drag in a *deus ex machina*. Let me think. We leave here together, we drive away, we have a terrible car-crash, you are crippled and hideously disfigured for life, once more I suffer a major amnesia, ten years later we meet again by chance and I fall in love with you in your wheelchair. For purely spiritual reasons, of course.'

He steals a look back at her face. It is turned away, against the pillow. The tears are over, but it has something of the grave inturnedness of a child's, after a tantrum; that sad first consciousness of what adulthood will bring. When she speaks it is in a quiet, cool voice.

'I rather thought you were trying to preserve the classical unities.'

'With Erato, yes. But now we've dropped her ...'

'It seems terribly contrived to me. A car-crash.'

'Then how about one of those spendidly inconclusive endings?'

Again she is slow to answer.

'I'm not quite sure what you mean.'

'Here we are. It hasn't worked. We show how splendidly mature and contemporary we are by agreeing it hasn't worked. We dress, we walk out ... I begin to see it, I like it. We walk out, we leave the hospital, we cross the fore-court, we stop in the street. Just a man and a woman, in a world where nothing works anyway. We can't even find the two taxis we need. Not that we'd really mind, we'd both be so enormously relieved at the thought that we were never going to see each other again. You'd say "Well ... " and I'd say something trite in reply, like "Well" as well. We'd smile briefly and wryly at our banality, then shake hands. Turn our backs, walk quickly away in opposite directions. Perhaps I might sneak one last glance back, but you'd already have disappeared for eternity among the passing throng and the stench of traffic pollution. I wouldn't have to spell out a moral. I go into a future mercifully without imagination. You go into a future mer-cifully without existence. How does that sound?' But he goes on before she can answer. 'The critics would love it. They adore downbeat endings. It shows how brave they are leading upbeat lives themselves.'

She says nothing for a long moment. Then she raises herself on an elbow, and touches a last small wetness from her eyes.

'I suppose you couldn't imagine some cigarettes – and a lighter and ashtray?'

He stands, like some remiss host. 'Of course. Any particular brand?'

'I have a feeling I'd be rather fond of Turkish, actually.'

'Some grass?'

She shakes her head quickly. 'No no. I'm sure I've been through that phase.'

'Right.'

He gives three quick snaps of thumb and forefinger. Instantly an onyx ashtray, a gold lighter, a silver cigarette-box appear on the bed beside her; so instantly, that she starts back a little. She picks an oval cigarette out of the box. Leaning across, he picks up the lighter and holds the flame out for her. She breathes out smoke, then holds the cigarette away with cocked wrist. 'Thanks.'

Clutching the bathrobe across her breasts, she shifts and sits upright; then tucks it securely under her armpits. He bends solicitously.

'Anything else?'

She gives his inquiring face a shy, faintly rueful glance. 'Well actually . . . would it be asking too much? As a matter of fact I seem to be the teeniest bit shortsighted.'

'My dear girl, you should have said. Any particular sort of frame?'

She inhales on her cigarette, staring at the door, then breathes the smoke out; another shy glance at him.

'I think I'd usually wear those blue-tinted ones with large circular lenses. Just a thin gold rim. Opticians call them "Jane Austen", I believe.'

'Like this?'

His hand holds out the glasses.

'That's super. Most kind.' She puts them on, adjusts the earpieces, then looks up at him with an embarrassed smile. 'So silly. All these ridiculous petty details.'

'Not at all. Anything else?'

'Only if it wouldn't be any trouble.'

'Please.'

'It's just this green.' She touches the bathrobe. 'I suspect it's not quite me.'

'Choose.'

'Something wine-dark? The colour of mulberry juice? I don't know if you remember that passage in Proust ... oh that's lovely. Perfect. Exactly what I had in mind. Thank you so much.'

'Coffee?'

'No.' She waves the cigarette sideways. 'This is fine.'

'No trouble. Just another couple of lines.'

'Really. Thanks all the same.'

She smokes for a few moments in silence, contemplating her bare feet below the hem of the new robe. He sits on the chair. At last she looks up with a diffident smile.

'Miles, I don't want to start another argument – may I call you Miles?'

'Please.'

'You were kind enough a minute ago to suggest that even though I don't really exist, I might from now on be allowed some say – I think you said consultation – in our relationship.'

'Absolutely. What you said about certain elementary freedoms ... point taken.'

'Except – I mean forgive me for harking back to a hatchet we've both agreed to bury, but you do still rather seem to be laying down the law about our mutual future.'

'That was the last thing I intended. It was simply an idea. Wide open to discussion. You don't like it?'

She smoothes the robe.

'It's just that I should have thought you would have made your point more validly by regarding what's happened so far as a kind of surrealistic preamble – if you like, a reversal of normal narrative development – to a very different kind of relationship between us in a much more realistic external context.' She smoothes the robe again over her legs. 'One where we would meet quite normally and develop a casual sort of friendship. I mean, obviously, well this side of ever going to bed together. We'd perhaps go to the theatre occasionally. Discuss books. Visit art exhibitions. That sort of thing.'

'Ah.'

'I'd just like to suggest that since all the boring bed scenes would have taken place in the fantasy preamble, you could then institute a much cooler and more contemporary tone and concentrate on the really serious and adult things. Our cultural backgrounds. Politics. Issues like abortion and street violence. Nuclear disarmament. Ecology. Whales. White bread. Whatever it was that prevented us from fully committing to each other.'

'That subtler nuances of so much liberal *Angst*?'

'Precisely.'

'You see a ... cultural background for yourself?'

'I think I'd like to be ... well, perhaps a graduate in English? Cambridge? I feel I might have written one or two commercially not very successful but in certain circles quite widely respected books of poetry. Something like that. I'd probably be an associate editor with one of the literary magazines.'

'A very laid-back, fastidious, morally scrupulous sort of girl?'

'If you don't think it's too vain. Too improbable.'

'Not at all.'

She looks modestly down. 'Thank you.'

'And me?'

She taps the cigarette into the onyx ashtray. 'Well, I rather see you as one of those well-to-do businessmen with vaguely artistic interests. Not quite knowing what to make of me, or my milieu, or anything really, outside your office. And making money. I suppose I mean baffled, even frightened by me and my greater sophistication, the much more intellectual world I work in. You know?' She adds quickly, 'Purely to form a realistic contrast with this. Of course.'

'I see.'

She looks at him a moment through her blue-tinted lenses, then raises a hand and touches down her tousled hair, then tucks the robe discreetly in again.

'Miles, I'd just like to say one thing, while we are being more open with each other. I feel I was rather unnecessarily emotional and outspoken a few minutes ago. I do have some sympathy with your problems. Especially as I realize I constitute one of them. I know the overwhelming stress the prevailing capitalist hegemony puts on sexuality. How difficult it is to escape.' She draws up her knees and sits with her legs slightly curled, sideways, beneath the purple robe. Then she gives him a frank, if faintly owlish look through her spectacles. 'I'm trying to say, of course do do it your way. If you feel mine's too difficult for you. It well may be.'

'I'd like to have a stab at it.'

'I'm seriously not insisting.'

'I think you're being extraordinarily generous over the mess I've made of it.'

'I know there has to be give and take.'

'Except so far I've done all the taking.'

She shrugs. 'But as technically I don't exist . . . '

'But you do. You've just shown you've a will of your own.'

She makes a little downward *moue*, self-deprecating. 'Hardly a will, I'm afraid. Just a whisper of an instinct.'

There is silence for a moment or two. Again she smoothes the purple towelling.

'This really is a heavenly colour. I adore bruised purple.'

'Good.'

She pauses, then resumes the more serious train of their conversation.

'I also don't want you to feel guilty about the ... taking. I'm not totally blind to biological realities. I'd hate you to think I'm just one more blue-stocking. Certain of your caresses – you must have realized. What you made me do in the beginning, in spite of myself I ... something in me was stirred.'

'I think that makes it even worse. I was simply taking advantage of your being normally female.'

'I was just as bad. That story about the satyr ... ' she covers her eyes in self-distaste.

'I provoked it.'

'I know, but I embroidered it terribly. When I ought to have resisted telling it at all. I do hope you'll always cut that particular passage out, if you ever ... you know.'

'It was all my fault.'

'It takes two.'

'You're being much too hard on yourself.'

'I honestly don't think I am.' She goes back to smoothing the robe again, over her knee. 'It was just the way you threw me in at the deep end. Sexually. It caught me off balance. I somehow simply realized, from the very first page of my existence, that I was basically rather a shy person, despite being apparently quite attractive to men.'

'Very attractive.'

'Seriously, I'd rather just be "quite". Not perhaps without a certain hint of underlying sensuality, but definitely nothing too *voulu*. The sort of person who has to be aroused very slowly and gently.'

'I understand.'

She keeps her eyes lowered. 'What I really want to say is that I think I would be prepared to accept some compromise about the nature of our relationship in the eventual future, if you insisted. When we knew each other better.'

'You mean the one where you're the highbrow lady poet and I'm the crass businessman?'

She gives him a quickly anxious look, full of aghast sincerity.

'Please, I didn't say that at all, Miles. Not crass. If you were, that, obviously I ... my character wouldn't look at you. A perfectly nice man in his way. Just a little ... limited and deformed by his milieu and profession.'

'I'm not absolutely clear what compromise you had in mind.'

'If you would prefer them to ... well, to put it quite, quite baldly, have a rather more overtly physical relationship in the end.'

'To make it?'

'If you want to put it that way.'

'I sort of saw her as too choosy for that.'

'Oh I think she would be for a long time. Certainly for many chapters. Perhaps to the very end.'

'The climax?'

She looks down, but with the trace of a prim smile.

'You're incorrigible.'

'It wasn't intended.'

'I'm sure it was. But never mind.'

'I still can't quite see how it would happen. Given the basic character premise.'

'That's really not for me to say. Your department.'

'I want it to be yours as well.'

She looks down. 'It seems so absurd. Like teaching one's

grandmother to suck eggs. You must have had so much more experience. I feel so terribly conscious I'm only a few pages old.'

'Never mind. You're learning fast.'

'Spare my blushes.'

'Not at all. I mean it.'

She leaves a little silence, then slips him a look.

'You're absolutely sure?'

'Absolutely.'

She stubs out her cigarette. 'Then just out of my head, very much off the cuff ... I suppose some crisis in the relationship, your becoming more and more desperate for me, your wanting to leave your wife for me –'

'Which wife is this?'

She glances up, surprised. 'I just imagined you'd be married. It's how I see you.'

'So long as I know.'

She folds her arms and stares at the door. 'Anyway, one hot summer night you come round to my Knightsbridge flat to thrash it all out one last time, why you love me, why I ought to love you, and so on, and by chance I've gone to bed early and have only a short nightdress on.' She hesitates a moment, then twitches at the robe. 'Or this. Whatever. It's very close, there's thunder in the air, I don't want to let you in, but you insist, and suddenly somehow everything boils over, your previous diffidence becomes dark desire, your manhood is at last inflamed, without a word you spring and tear the flimsy garment from my bare shoulders, I scream and struggle, I half escape, I manage to stagger to the french windows and out into the steamy pouring rain, you –'

'It's a ground-floor flat?'

'Yes, of course. Obviously.'

'I was just worried about the neighbours, if you scream.'

'All right, I hiss low words of passionate hatred. I haven't worked out all the minutiae, Miles.'

'Sorry. I interrupted.'

'It is the first time I've ever done this.'

'I'm sorry.'

'I've forgotten where I was.'

'Just outside the french windows. In the steamy pouring rain.'

'I run on to the lawn, but you're much too agile and strong, too animal, and you catch me and throw me on the soft turf, I twist and wrestle, you take brutal possession of me against my will, I weep as your pent-up lust ravages my deepest principles.' She leaves a little pause. 'I'm only giving you the rough idea.'

'I like the soft turf. The only thing is, I thought . . . '

'Yes?'

'You did say something about slow and gentle arousal.'

She gives him a touchingly delicate and hurt look, and speaks in a lower voice, her eyes down.

'I'm female, Miles. I can't help being a tissue of contradictions.'

'Of course. Forgive me.'

'I mean, obviously you'd have to prepare for this moment of sexual violence. You might for instance show me as I undress before you come, a moment when I might look at myself naked in some mirror and secretly wonder whether poetry is enough.'

'I'll certainly bear that in mind.'

'You could even show me sadly taking down my copy of Nicholas Chorier from my bookshelves.'

'Nicholas who?'

'Possibly I'm being a tiny bit *recherchée*. The passage I had in mind was the *deuxième dialogue*. *Tribadicon*, as he rather coarsely entitled it. Lyons, 1658.' She gives him an inquiring shake of her head. 'No?'

'No.'

'I'm sorry. I somehow assumed you would have all the pornographic classics by heart.'

'Might I ask how, in your few pages of existence, you happen to –'

'Oh Miles!' She gives a hurried smile down. 'Really. I thought we were speaking outside the illusions of text.' She looks up again. 'I mean, take just that one time when, as Dr Delfie, I asked you why you didn't just get off the bed and leave the room. In reality you took six weeks before you could find an answer. I had to do something while I waited. I felt that at the very least I should familiarize myself with the kind of book evidently dearest to your heart.' She adds, 'As your employee. So to speak.'

'That was very conscientious of you.'

'Not at all.'

'To wade through all that appalling filth.'

'Miles, I couldn't face life if I wasn't conscientious about my work. I'm afraid it's my nature. I can't help it. I'm an over-achiever.'

He watches her. She is looking down at the bed again, as if embarrassed to have to expound herself so seriously.

'We left ourselves in the rain in the garden. What next?'

'I think it might turn out that I'd been dying for you to do something like that for chapters on end, but of course I was far too complex emotionally to realize it. I'm weeping for joy really. At last I know orgasm.'

'In the rain?'

'If you don't think it's *de trop*. Moonlight, if you prefer.'

He sits back a little.

'And one ends on that?'

She peers gravely at him through the owlish glasses.

'Miles, one can hardly end a contemporary novel on the implication that mere fucking solves anything.'

'Of course not.'

She smoothes the robe again. 'Actually I see that scene as the finale of the first part of a trilogy.'

'Stupid of me not to guess.'

She picks at a loose thread in the robe towelling.

'In the second part of which I think I'd probably become a total victim of my hitherto repressed sensuality. A Messalina *de nos jours*, as it were. I know you could do this middle section in your sleep.'

'I must have misunderstood. Weren't all the boring bed scenes to go into the Alice-in-Wonderland preamble?'

'I sincerely hope these wouldn't be boring. Of course I get no pleasure from it all. I'm only doing it out of despair.'

'Despair of what?'

She looks at him over her glasses. 'I'm supposed to be a twentieth-century woman, Miles. By definition I'm in despair.'

'And what becomes of my character?'

She takes another cigarette from the box.

'You'd become terrribly jealous, you'd start drinking, your business would go to pot. In the end you'd have to live on my immoral earnings. You'd become haggard, bearded, a broken shell of the . . . ' she pauses to light her cigarette ' . . . successful banana importer you once were.'

'I was once what!'

She blows a plume of smoke.

'It has a number of advantages.'

'I have no ambition whatever to be a banana importer.'

'I think you might be a touch colourless without a slightly exotic background. As a matter of fact I see our very first meeting in the real world taking place in one of your East End ripening sheds. Our oblique and tentative dialogue counterpointed by those vistas of thousands of detumescent vegetable penises.'

'I'm not sure I'd know how to write that.'

'I'd hate to lose it.' She pauses. 'It feels right.'

'It feels right?'

'Feeling right is terribly important to me, Miles.' She gives him the hurt ghost of a prim smile. 'I'd rather hoped you'd realized that by now.'

He takes a slight breath. 'And the third part of this trilogy?'

'I was going to be more specific about one or two scenes in the second. When the unnatural female animal in me takes over. There was one with two Dutch car salesmen and a lecturer in Erse that I –'

'I think I'd prefer a general synopsis. For now.'

'All right. Well.' She cocks the wrist of the hand holding the cigarette. 'I'm sure you've noticed a missing element in the first two parts. No?'

'I'm afraid not.'

'Religion.'

'Religion?'

'I think I should become a nun. There could be scenes at the Vatican. They always sell well.'

He stares at the old rose carpet beneath the bed.

'I thought we were a fiercely fastidious Cambridge graduate in English.'

'That's where the pathos would be. When someone who has sat at the feet of the Leavises and Dr Steiner is brutally raped by –'

'And you do seem awfully hooked on brutality, if you don't mind my saying so.'

She lowers her glasses again and looks at him over them.

'I understood it was generally agreed that any accurate mimesis of contemporary reality must reflect symbolically the brutality of class relations in a bourgeois-dominated society.'

'When you put it like that. And who ...?'

'Twenty-four young black Marxist guerrillas in my African mission-house. There'd be a place for your character. He could come to Rome for the beatification ceremony. With his new lover.'

'I thought I loved you.'

She exhales smoke.

'Obviously not after I took my vows. It wouldn't be *vraisemblable*.'

'And where does this other woman come from?'

'I wasn't talking about a woman, Miles.'

'You mean ...'

'After the shock of losing me to God, I think your true sexual nature might very plausibly declare itself.'

'But –'

'Quite apart from the fact, which I'm sure you know, that gay readers now constitute 13·8 per cent of all English-speaking fiction buyers. Not that that would influence you. But it is a point.'

She goes back to picking at the loose thread.

'But why on earth should a homosexual want to go to your beatification ceremony?'

'Because you can't forget me. Besides, I expect you and your hair-dressing friend would love the high camp of it all. The incense and vestments. Actually it might be rather nice if we ended with your confusing my face – after I'm dead, of course – with that of a statue of the Virgin Mary in your own local church.'

'I'm a Catholic too, now?'

'From the first. I forgot to tell you.' She looks up at him. 'You must have one character. And a sense of sin. They're 28·3 per cent.'

'Catholics?'

She nods. 'And I have an interesting idea for a very last scene. I see you secretly placing a little hand of unripe bananas at the foot of my statue – or her statue. I think it might be particularly meaningful to end on that.'

'What the devil's it supposed to mean?'

She has a demurely patronizing smile.

'Don't worry. I think your more discriminating readers would grasp the symbolism.'

'Isn't a bunch of vegetable penises a bit blasphemous, in the circumstances?'

'Not if you offered them on your knees, with tears in your eyes.'

'You don't think I might have dropped one banana at the top of the steep flight of steps leading up to this church?'

'Why?'

'When I come out after the *ex voto* bit I could slip on it.'

She looks at him for a moment, then down. There is a silence. Then she speaks in a small, hurt voice.

'I was only trying to help.'

'I didn't mean anything funny. Naturally I'd break my spine on the way down.'

'I was simply trying to find the sort of general framework that might give scope to your talents. As I understand them.' She shrugs, eyes still down, and stubs out her cigarette. 'It doesn't matter. I don't really care.'

He goes and sits on the side of the bed, turned towards her.

'I can see it has all sorts of possibilities.'

'You don't sound very convinced.'

'Seriously. It's amazing how you open up a whole new world in a few broad brushstrokes.'

She gives him a hesitant, doubting look, then lowers her head again.

III

'I think you think it's just silly.'

'Not at all. Very instructive. I feel I know you ten times better now.'

'It was only a brief outline.'

'They're often the most revealing.'

She gives him another look through the huge blue-smoked lenses.

'I know you could do it, Miles. If you really tried.'

'One or two minor points still puzzle me slightly. May I . . .?'

'Please.'

'For instance, why *twenty-four* black guerrillas?'

'It seems the right sort of number. Not that I'm an expert, naturally. You'd have to research that.'

'It's also the number of letters in the Greek alphabet.'

'Is it? I'd forgotten.' He stares at her. She shakes her head. 'I'm sorry. I don't quite see the relevance.'

'Perhaps there isn't.'

'I don't see how there could be. Frankly.'

'And have you by any chance thought of a name for this emotionally very complex female character of yours?'

She reaches out and touches his wrist. 'I'm so glad you mentioned that. I don't want you to feel I'm rejecting all your ideas. Actually, Erato might be just the thing. It's unusual. I think we should retain that.'

'You don't think it's pretty far-fetched? Naming a con-temporary character after a very obscure minor divinity, who never existed in the first place?'

'I think it's rather charmingly enigmatic.'

'But surely it would appeal only to the point zero zero one per cent of our hopeful readership who have even heard her name, let alone know who she was – or rather, wasn't?'

'Every little counts, Miles.'

He leans across her, supporting himself on an arm,

bringing their faces much closer. His eyes are reflected in the smoke-blue lenses. She draws back, hitching the robe higher.

'I have one final question.'

'Yes?'

'How long is it since your impudent little Greek bottom was last tanned?'

'Miles!'

'Erato.'

'I thought we were getting on so well.'

'*You* were getting on so well.'

He removes her glasses, and stares at her. The face looks strangely young now, without the glasses; not a day over twenty, and as innocent as something half that age. She lowers her eyes, then murmurs, 'You wouldn't dare. I'd never forgive you.'

'Just try me. Just inspire me with one more helpful literary suggestion.'

She hitches her robe up again, and looks sideways and downwards.

'I'm sure she'd have thought of something better. If she did exist.'

'And don't you dare start that again.' He forces her face up and round, so that she has to look him in the eyes. 'And don't give me that butter-wouldn't-melt look over your ineffably classical nose.'

'Miles, you're hurting me.'

'Good. Now listen. You may be a goddess of a very inferior and fifth-rate kind. You may be quite a good-looking goddess as goddesses go. Or go-go. You are also your father's child. In plain language, a by-blow of the randiest old goat in all theology. There is not the tiniest shred of modesty in your entire make-up. Your mind is indistinguishable from that of a 1920s vamp. My true error is not to have got you up as Theda Bara.' He shifts the angle of the face a little. 'Or Dietrich in *The Blue Angel*.'

'Miles, please . . . I don't know what's come over you.'

'Your astounding chutzpah has come over me.' He taps the classical nose. 'I know your game. You are simply trying to spin out an erotic situation beyond all the bounds of artistic decency.'

'Miles, you're beginning to frighten me.'

'What you'd really like is for me to tear away that robe and leap on top of you again. If you had the strength I bet you'd leap on top of me instead.'

'Now you're being horrid.'

'And the only reason you are not over my knees and getting the belting of your life is that I know you'd like nothing better.'

'That's a beastly thing to say.'

He taps her nose again. 'The game's up, my girl. You've played it once too often.'

He leans away, then flicks a thumb and finger imperiously at the chair beside the bed. As instantly as before a light-weight summer suit on a hanger appears on it; a shirt, tie, socks, underclothes; a pair of shoes between its front legs. He stands.

'I'm going to get dressed now. And you're going to listen.' He dons the shirt, then turns to look at her as he buttons it. 'You needn't think I don't know what's behind all this. It's pure pique on your side. You can't bear to see me come up with a good idea of my own. And what your exceedingly feeble imitation of a bookish young woman failed totally to hide is your astounding ignorance of what contemporary literature is about. I bet you haven't even cottoned on to what these grey quilted walls really stand for.' He pauses in the buttoning and looks at her. She shakes her head. 'I knew you hadn't. Grey walls, grey cells.

114

Grey matter?' He taps the side of his head. 'Does the drachma begin to drop?'

'It's all . . . taking place inside your brain?'

'Brilliant.'

She looks round the walls, up at the domed ceiling, then back at him. 'I never realized.'

'Now we're getting somewhere.' He stoops to pull on his underpants. 'The amnesia?'

'I . . . I thought it was just a way of . . . '

'Of what?'

'Giving yourself an excuse to write a bit of soft –'

'And we see ourself as a graduate in English. Jesus.' He turns and takes the trousers from the hanger. 'You'll be telling me next you've never even heard of Todorov.'

'Of who?'

'You haven't, have you?'

'I'm afraid not, Miles. I'm sorry.'

He faces her again, holding the trousers out. 'How can one possibly discuss theory with you when you haven't even read the basic texts?'

'Tell me.'

He pulls the trousers on. 'Well . . . in simple layman's language, the whole delicate symbolism of the amnesia derived from the ambiguous nature, in both its hypostatic and epiphanic *facies*, of the diegetic processus. Especially in terms of the anagnorisis.' He begins tucking in his shirt. 'Thus Dr Delfie.'

'Dr Delfie?'

'Obviously.'

'Obviously what, Miles?'

'The futility of trying to deal with it causally.'

'I thought she was trying to deal with it sexually.'

He looks up impatiently from tucking in the shirt.

'The sex was just a metaphor, for heaven's sake. There

has to be some kind of objective correlative for the herme-neutical side of it. Even a child could see that.'

'Yes, Miles.'

He does up the zip. 'It's too late now.' He sits down and begins to pull on his socks.

'I honestly didn't realize.'

'Of course not. There was an absolutely first-class final couple of pages to come. Two of the best I'd have ever written. If you hadn't blundered in like a bloody elephant.'

'Miles, I'm not even nine stone.'

He glances up, with a humourlessly long-suffering grimace. 'Look, my love, your body's all right. It's just your mind. It's at least three hundred years out of date.'

'There's no need to be so angry about it.'

'I'm not angry. I'm just pointing out one or two things for your own good.'

'Everyone's so dreadfully serious these days.'

He wags a finger, and the sock the other fingers are holding, at her. 'I'm glad you brought that up. That's another thing. There may be a place for humour in ordinary life, but there is none whatever for it in serious modern fiction. I don't mind wasting an occasional hour strictly in private with you exchanging the kind of badinage you seem so fond of. But if I ever let that sort of thing creep into my published texts, my reputation would turn to ashes over-night.' She sits with her eyes cast down under this tirade. He bends to put on his sock, and goes on slightly less harshly. 'It's a question of priorities. I know you were brought up as a pagan, and you can't help that. Nor I suppose can you help being landed with a much more profound and difficult field for inspiration than you ever bargained for, though I'm bound to say I think it was a grave mistake picking on someone whose only previous experience was with love ditties. The obvious candidate for the modern novel was your sister Melpomene. I can't think why she wasn't chosen. But that's spilt milk.'

She speaks in a very small voice. 'May I ask something?'

He stands, and picks up the tie from the back of the chair.

'Of course.'

'I can't quite understand, if there's a place for humour in ordinary life, why there can't also be one in the novel. I thought it was meant to reflect life.'

He leaves the tie hanging untied round his neck, and puts his hands on his hips.

'Oh God. I honestly don't know where to begin with you.' He bends forward slightly. 'The reflective novel is sixty years dead, Erato. What do you think modernism was about? Let alone post-modernism. Even the dumbest students know it's a *reflexive* medium now, not a reflective one. Do you even know what *that* means?'

She shakes her head, avoiding his eyes. What she pretended in the story of the satyr seems at present to be taking place literally; she looks not a day over seventeen, a high-school student being forced to confess that she has not done her homework. He leans forward, tapping one extended forefinger with the other.

'Serious modern fiction has only one subject: the difficulty of writing serious modern fiction. First, it has fully accepted that it is only fiction, can only be fiction, will never be anything but fiction, and therefore has no business at all tampering with real life or reality. Right?'

He waits. She nods meekly.

'Second. The natural consequence of this is that writing *about* fiction has become a far more important matter than writing fiction itself. It's one of the best ways you can tell the true novelist nowadays. He's not going to waste his time over the messy garage-mechanic drudge of assembling stories and characters on paper.'

She looks up. 'But –'

'Yes, all right. Obviously he has at some point to write something, just to show how irrelevant and unnecessary the actual writing part of it is. But that's all.' He starts tying his tie. 'I'm putting this in the simplest terms for you. Are you with me so far?'

She nods. He ties his tie.

'Third, and most important. At the creative level there is in any case no connection whatever between author and text. They are two entirely separate things. Nothing, but nothing, is to be inferred or deduced from one to the other, and in either direction. The deconstructivists have proved that beyond a shadow of doubt. The author's role is purely fortuitous and agential. He has no more significant a status than the bookshop assistant or the librarian who hands the text *qua* object to the reader.'

'Why do writers still put their names on the title-page, Miles?' She looks timidly up. 'I'm only asking.'

'Because most of them are like you. Quite incredibly behind the times. And hair-raisingly vain. Most of them are still under the positively medieval illusion that they write their own books.'

'I honestly didn't realize.'

'If you want story, character, suspense, description, all that antiquated nonsense from pre-modernist times, then go to the cinema. Or read comics. You do not come to a serious modern writer. Like me.'

'No, Miles.'

He realizes something has gone wrong with the knot of his tie; and rather irritatedly pulls it apart, then starts the tying again.

'Our one priority now is mode of discourse, function of

discourse, status of discourse. Its metaphoricality, its disconnectedness, its totally ateleological self-containedness.'

'Yes, Miles.'

'I know you thought you were half-teasing just now, but I consider it symptomatic of your ridiculously outdated views. You really haven't a hope of inspiring anything worth even doctorate-level analysis when your first thought is always the same: how quickly you can get people's clothes off and have them hop into bed. It's absurd. Like thinking bow-and-arrow in the age of the neutron bomb.' He surveys her bent head. 'I know you're a harmless enough creature at heart and I do feel a certain affection for you. Actually you'd have made an excellent geisha girl. But you have got most terribly and hopelessly out of touch. Before you started interfering today the sexual component was absolutely clinical – if I may say so, rather cleverly deprived of all eroticism.' He pulls down the shirt collar, and gives the better knot of the second tying a last little tightening. 'Clearly metaphysical in intent, at least to academic readers, who are the only ones who count nowadays. Then in you come, the whole neatly balanced structure's blown to smithereens, it all has to be flogged to death, sent up, trivialized, adulterated to suit the vulgarest mass-market taste. It's ruined now. Quite impossible. Is my tie straight?'

'Yes. And I'm terribly sorry.'

He sits again to put on his shoes.

'Look, I'll be quite candid, Erato. Let's face it, this isn't the first time by any means we've had this sort of time-wasting trouble together. I'm not denying you can be quite helpful over one or two elementary aspects of the so-called female mind – inasmuch as the fundamental preoccupation of the modern novel still unfortunately has to be mediated through various superficial masks and props, alias men and women. But I don't think you've ever understood the creative mind. You're like a certain kind of editor. In the end you always want to write the whole damned book yourself. It's just not on. I mean, if you want to write books, go off and write them yourself. You easily could, there's a growing audience for a certain kind of women's novel these days. "He rammed his four-letter thing up my four-letter thing" – that sort of stuff.' He gives his shoe-laces a final firm pull. 'Read Jong.'

'The Swiss psychologist?'

'Never mind. The point is this. You must learn to accept that for me, for all of us who are truly serious, you can never again be more than occasional editorial adviser in one or two very secondary areas.' He stands and reaches for his suit-jacket. 'And I must in all frankness tell you that you're not even very reliable at that any more. You still go on as if the world's a pleasant place to live in. There's no more flagrant give-away of superficiality of approach to life in general. Every internationally admired and really successful modern artist of recent times has shown it's totally pointless, black and absurd. Complete hell.'

'Even when you're internationally admired and really successful, Miles?'

He stands looking down at the bent head. 'That is a very childish and cheap remark.'

'I'm sorry, Miles.'

'Are you doubting the sincerity of some of the tragic key figures of contemporary culture?'

'No, Miles. Of course not.'

He is silent for a moment, to let his disapproval sink in; then continues in an even more critical voice.

'It's all very well your making dubious jokes about twentieth-century womankind being by definition in des-pair. The fact is, you'd rather die than not be a woman yourself. You love every minute of it. You wouldn't recognize genuine despair if it fell off the roof and hit you on the head.'

'Miles, I can't help that.'

'All right. Then be a woman, and enjoy it. But don't try to think in addition. Just accept that that's the way the biological cards have fallen. You can't have a male brain and intellect as well as a mania for being the universal girl-friend. Does that sound unreasonable?'

'Not if you say so, Miles.'

'Good.' He puts on his jacket. 'Now I suggest we forget this whole unfortunate episode and shake hands. Then I'll leave you here. At some future date, when and if I feel I could use a little advice, I'll give you a ring. No offence, but I'll call you. And I suggest that next time we meet in a public place. I'll take you to some kebab house for lunch, we'll talk, we'll drink a little retsina, we'll behave like two civilized contemporary people. If I have time I'll take you to the airport, put you on the plane back to Greece. And that'll be that. Okay?' She nods meekly. 'And one last thing. I also think I'd be happier if in future we operate on a financial basis. I'll give you a little fee for anything I use, right? I can always claim it against tax as research.'

She nods again. He watches her a moment, then stretches out his hand, which she takes and shakes limply. He hesitates, then bends and kisses the top of her head, and briefly pats a bare shoulder.

'Cheer up, old girl. You'll get over it. It had to be said.'

'Thank you for being so frank.'

'Not at all. Part of the room-service. Now. Is there anything you'd like before I go? Some pretty clothes? A magazine? *Woman's Own? Good Housekeeping? Vogue?*'

'It's all right. I'll manage.'

'Only too happy to call a taxi on my way out.' She shakes

her head. 'You're sure?' She nods. 'And no hard feelings?'
She shakes her head again. He smiles, almost avuncularly.
'These are the 1980s.'

'I know.'

He reaches a hand and ruffles the Grecian hair. 'Then
'ciao.'

''Ciao.'

He turns and starts walking towards the door, with a
firm tread and the demeanour of someone looking forward
to his next engagement, after having brought off an excellent business deal. *Mann ist was er isst*, and also what he
wears. Miles Green looks twice, ten times the man of the
world in his well-cut suit, his old school tie; not of course
(these are the 1980s) in the least ashamed at having found
time in a busy day to spend an hour or so with what is,
after all, essentially a mere call-girl; but now going on,
refreshed, to more serious matters – a meeting with his
agent, perhaps, or a literary conference, or the blessedly
masculine peace of his club. For the first time there is a
sense of rightness in the room, of sane reality.

Alas, it disappears almost as soon as it is come. Halfway
to the door, the buoyant tread freezes. It is immediately
clear why: there is no longer a door one can be halfway to.
Where it was, now stretches an unbroken wall of grey
quilting; even the hook has vanished. He flashes a look
back at the bed, but the chided figure there sits with her
head still bowed, transparently unaware of this minor
change of ambience. He looks back at where the door has
been; then flicks his thumb and finger at it. The wall
remains unchanged. Again; again nothing happens. He
hesitates, then strides to the place and begins groping the
quilting, as if he is blind and somewhere on it there must
be a handle. He stops, he steps back two or three paces,
almost as if getting ready to shoulder-charge. Instead, he

reaches his hands in front of him, a man sizing an imaginary door he is about to lift to its hinges. Once more there is the sound of a thumb and finger being clicked. Once more the wall remains exactly, blankly, doorlessly as it is. He gives the place on the wall a grim stare. Then he turns and marches back to the end of the bed.

'You can't do this!'

Very slowly her head comes up.

'No, Miles.'

'I'm in charge here.'

'Yes, Miles.'

'If you think anyone would believe this for a millionth of a second ... I order you to replace that door.' Her only answer is to recline against the pillows. 'Did you hear what I said?'

'Yes, Miles. I'm very stupid, but I have perfect hearing.'

'Then do what you're told.'

She raises her arms and locks her hands behind the slender neck. The bathrobe sags. She grins.

'I adore you when you pretend to be angry.'

'If that door is not back, and within five seconds, I warn you I shall start using physical violence.'

'Like the dear marquis.'

He takes a deep breath. 'You're behaving like a five-year-old.'

'Ah well. I am only a fifth-rate goddess.'

He stares at her, or rather at her bitten underlip.

'You cannot keep me here against my will.'

'And you can't walk out of your own brain.'

'Oh yes I can. It's only my metaphorical brain. You're being totally absurd. You might just as well cancel the laws of nature, or make time go backwards.'

'I do, Miles. Quite often. If you remember.'

And suddenly every stitch he has just put on vanishes.

123

He moves his hands hastily and instinctively in front of him. She bites her lips again.

'I'm not going to stand for this!'

She pats the bed beside her. 'Then why don't you come and sit down?'

He turns away and folds his arms. 'Never.'

'Your poor little thing. I wish you'd let me kiss it.' He stares even more grimly into space – or what little the room allows. She takes the purple bathrobe and tosses it lightly towards him at the foot of the bed. 'Would you like this? I don't need it any more.'

He glances resentfully down at the robe, then snatches it up. It is too small for him, but he manages to force it on and pull the front flaps across and tie the belt. Then he strides to the chair, grabs it up, walks to the corner of the room and firmly plants it by the table with its back to the bed. He sits with arms folded and legs crossed; and stares resolutely at the corner of the quilted room, five feet away. There is a silence. At last he speaks over his shoulder.

'You may take my clothes away, you may stop me leaving. You cannot change my feelings.'

'I know. You silly thing.'

'Then this is a ridiculous waste of time.'

'Unless you change them yourself.'

'Never.'

'Miles.'

'In your own words, one has to have some elementary freedoms to exist.'

She sits watching him, then suddenly gets off the bed and looks underneath it, and retrieves the chaplet of roses and myrtle-leaves. She faces the wall, as if there were a mirror there, and sets it back in place, adjusts it a little, and plays for a moment with her hair, flicking out one or two dark curls; and at last satisfied with her appearance, speaks across the room to him.

'May I come and sit on your lap, Miles?'

'You may not.'

'Please.'

'No.'

'I'll be only fifteen if you like.'

He swivels abruptly round and points a finger.

'You keep away.'

But she comes towards him. However, just short of where he sits, seemingly poised to spring at her if she advances a step closer, she kneels on the old rose carpet, crosses her hands over her lap, and sits back submissively on her heels. He bears those eyes for a moment or so, then looks away.

'I only gave you the seed of it. You did all the real work.'

He sits briefly in silence, then explodes.

'God, when I think of all that palaver about plasticine, about pashas and harems. And Hitler!' He whips round on her. 'You know something? You're the biggest little fascist in the whole of history. And you needn't think kneeling there with that dying spaniel look in your eyes fools me for one moment.'

'Fascists hate sex, Miles.'

He gives her a ghastly caricature of a smile. 'Even the worst philosophies have their good points.'

'And love.'

'I find that an obscene word in the circumstances.'

'And tenderness.'

'You're about as tender as a bloody cactus.'

'And they can never laugh at themselves.'

'I realize that destroying every belief a man has in himself, in effectively castrating him for the rest of his life, is a highly amusing situation. That you're being enormously self-restrained in not rolling on the floor at the sheer fun of it. You'll excuse me for not joining in.'

'All this just because you realize that after all you do need me a little?'

'I do not need you. The only need in it is yours. To humiliate me.'

'Miles.'

'I meant every word I said just then. You've ruined my work from the start, with your utterly banal, pifflingly novelettish ideas. I hadn't the least desire to be what I am when I began. I was going to follow in Joyce's and Beckett's footsteps. But oh no, in you trot. Every female character has to be changed out of recognition. She must do this, must do that. Every time, pump her up till she swamps the whole shoot. And in the end it's always the same bloody one. I.e., you. Again and again you've made me cut out the best stuff. That text where I had twelve different endings – it was perfect as it was, no one had ever done that before. Then you get at it, and I'm left with just three. The whole point of the thing was missed. Wasted.' He turns to look angrily at her. She is biting her lips. 'I can tell you now where I'm setting the next one. Mount Athos.'

The smile deepens. He looks away and rants on.

'All you've ever done is dictate. I have about as much say as an automatic typewriter. God, when I think of the endless pages the French have spent on trying to decide whether the writer himself is written or not. Ten seconds with you would have proved that one for ever.'

'You know that's not true.'

'Then why can't that door go back? Why for once can't I end this the way I want? Why do you always have to have the last word?'

'Miles, now it's you who's not being very consistent.

You've just told me there's no connection at all between author and text. So what's it matter?'

'Because I have a right to establish my own non-connection at all in my own personal way.'

'I know I'm only your poor little brainless girl-friend, but I don't think that really bears logical analysis.'

'I'm not going to argue about matters that are completely above your head.'

She watches his half-turned back.

'I don't want us to stop until we're friends again. Till you let me sit on your lap and give you a little cuddle. And a kiss.'

'Oh for God's sake.'

'I am very fond of you. And I'm not laughing at you any more.'

'You're always laughing at me.'

'Miles, look at me.'

He casts her a suspicious glance; and she is not laughing. But once more he turns away, as if what he reads in her eyes is even worse than laughter. She sits in silence a moment, watching him, then speaks again.

'All right. There. The door's back.'

He glances sharply towards where it was; and now indeed is again. She stands and goes to it, and opens it.

'Come on. Come and see what's the other side.' She reaches out a hand towards him. 'It won't hurt you.'

He gets impatiently up and goes to the open doorway, ignoring her hand; and looks through – at the man in the purple bathrobe that is too small for him, at the slimly naked girl with the chaplet of roses and classical pubis, at the bed in the background behind, the cuckoo-clock with the ghostly white chiton still hanging from its corner, the grey quilted walls. All stands as in a mirror, or a Magritte. She gestures, inviting him to go through.

'Ridiculous.'

He turns angrily away. She closes the door, regards his back thoughtfully for a moment, then takes a step or two nearer, behind him.

'Don't be so mean. Come and lie on the bed with me.'

'No.'

'We won't talk. We'll just make love.'

'Not in a thousand years.'

She puts her hands behind her back.

'Then just as friends.'

'We're not friends. We're two people who happen to be locked in the same prison cell. Thanks to your insufferable female petty-mindedness.'

'I feel I owe you so much for what you've just told me. And now you won't let me repay you.'

'No thanks.'

Already meek, her voice grows wheedling. 'I know you secretly want me to, Miles.'

'You know nothing.'

'I want to do something to you that the Cretan women did to their husbands when they came back from the siege of Troy. To show how much they'd missed them. It was in the *Ur*-text, but it's a lacuna in all the surviving manuscripts.'

'You're impossible.'

'It's very wicked.'

'I am categorically not interested in the sexual perversions of ancient Crete.'

'I know you are really.' She leaves a little pause. 'You wouldn't be so scared to look me in the face otherwise.'

He jerks round. 'I am not in the least sc-'

It is only a small fist; but the right uppercut is delivered from deep by her waist, and not only with all the vigour of a young woman who, though not an athlete in the normal sense, evidently takes a pride in her general physical trim, but rather more surprisingly, with professional precision and timing, crisp to the point of the jaw. One might almost suspect it is not the first time she has delivered such a punch. Clearly it gains most effect from coming, like one of her father's allegedly preferred form of guided missile, so out of the blue. Mr Miles Green's head is knocked visibly back. His mouth drops open, his eyes glaze and lose focus, he wavers, then slowly sinks to his knees; tries for an unsteady moment to stand again; and finally, aided by a very firm heel-push from a bare and delicately arched left foot, keels over on the old rose carpet and lies inert.

III

But what persuades many that it is difficult to
prove the existence of divinity is this. They never
raise their minds above things apprehensible to
the senses, and are become so accustomed to not
considering anything without first imagining it
– a way of thinking applicable only to material
objects – that all that is unimaginable seems to
them unintelligible. This is manifest in the fact
that even the philosophers hold it for a maxim
in their schools that nothing can enter the mind
that has not first passed through the senses – in
which, however, it is certain that the concept of
divinity has never found a place. It seems to me
that those who try to use their imagination to
understand this concept behave exactly as if they
tried to use their eyes to hear sounds or smell
scents ...

René Descartes, *Discours de la Méthode*

Mnemosyne's daughter stares down at her victim, reflectively licking her still-clenched knuckles. After a few seconds, the traditional (if not on this occasion counted) ten, she steps over the body and walks briskly to the side of the bed, where she presses the bell. From instant boxer – the very moment her finger-tip touches the plastic stud – she becomes instant Dr Delfie again. The tunic, the pocket of pens, the name-label, the hair bound severely back (the chaplet has vanished, like the chiton on the clock) by the discreet wisp of black and white scarf, each detail is restored. And so also is the former cool severity of expression. She is no longer either tender or teasing.

And now, retransmogrified, she walks back to the prone man and kneels by him. Like a ringside doctor, she lifts a wrist to take its pulse. Then she leans over the face – he has collapsed sprawled on his back – and opens the lids of an eye clinically. Suddenly the door opens.

An elderly staff sister, evidently of the stern and no-nonsense kind, stands there. There is something about her, an air of peerless officiousness, of knowing better than anyone else in her world what that world is about, that tells all, even before she speaks. She stares down disapprovingly through bespectacled, humourless eyes. The doctor is evidently taken by surprise. Rather awkwardly, for one so generally graceful, she scrambles to her feet.

'Sister . . . I thought Nurse Cory was on duty.'

'So did I, doctor. As usual she's nowhere to be found.'

Her eyes flick down at the patient. 'And that's also as usual, I suppose.'

'I'm afraid so.'

'I'm short-staffed enough as it is. His sort cause more trouble than the whole of the rest of the ward put together.'

'If you could find a male nurse and a stretcher. We'd better get him back to bed.'

The staff sister gives a bleak nod, but still stands surveying the unconscious patient, as she might an unwashed bedpan.

'You know my opinion, doctor. They need hormone treatment. If not surgical intervention. That's how we'd have dealt with it in the old days.'

'I do know your views, sister, thank you. You were kind enough to communicate them to us at some length at the last ward meeting.'

The staff sister bristles.

'I have the safety of my nurses to consider.'

The doctor folds her arms.

'I am aware of that, too.'

'I sometimes wonder what Dr Bowdler would think if he were still alive. The things that go on now in this hospital in the name of medicine.'

'If you're referring to all the new advances –'

'Advances! I know what I'd call most of them. It grows more and more like Bedlam.'

'Would you please find a male nurse and a stretcher?'

The sister does not budge.

'You may think I'm an old fool, doctor, but let me inform you of something else. I've been meaning to speak about it. These walls. They're unscrubbable. There's filthy, disgusting dirt in every single crevice of them. They're crawling with septicaemia. It's a miracle to me that we haven't had epidemic after epidemic here.'

'I'll see if I can't arrange one for you, sister.'

This is too much. The staff sister leans angrily forward.

'And don't you come the sarcastic with me, young woman. I've had more clever little would-be specialists through my hands than you've had hot dinners. You think you know everything, your generation. I'd like to remind you that I was dealing with cases like this when you were still in nappies.'

'Sister –'

But the dragoness is unstoppable.

'Half the patients in this ward are no better than malingerers. The last thing they need is kid-glove treatment from half-baked young doctors hardly out of medical school who –'

'Sister, I know you're going through a difficult period of your –'

'That has nothing to with it!'

'If you go on like this I shall have to speak to Matron.'

No good: the sister draws herself proudly up.

'Mrs Thatcher happens to share my views. Both on discipline and antisepsis.'

'Is this meant to be an example of discipline?'

'Don't you talk discipline to me. This ward has gone to rack and ruin ever since you were assigned to it.'

'By which I presume you mean it's only half the concentration camp it was before I came.'

It is immediately apparent that this over-eager attacking move is into a trap. The sister shifts her gaze to a point beyond the doctor's head, and speaks with the dignified moderation of one about to plunge a knife into a hated colleague's back.

'Better a concentration camp than a strip-tease show.'

'What do you mean by that?'

The sister still fixes the far wall with her pin-like eyes.

'You needn't think I don't know what went on in the Demonstration Theatre the other afternoon.'

'What went on?'

'You know very well. It's all over the hospital.'

'I do *not* know.'

'Mr Lawrence's new mastectomy incision.'

'What about it?'

'I hear it was demonstrated with surgical crayon upon your naked bosoms.'

'He could hardly do it on my clothed ones.' The sister gives a profoundly sceptical sniff. 'I merely happened to be passing when he looked out for a volunteer subject.'

'Before twenty-four male students. If I am informed correctly.'

'So?'

The sister's eyes suddenly blaze – if a glaucous grey can blaze – upon the doctor's.

'I am told the last thing most of them appeared to be studying was the line of the incision.'

Dr Delfie smiles, but very thinly.

'Sister, I should go to the dispensary and ask for two thirty-milligram Dembutoprazil tablets. And while you're about it, perhaps you could also do what I originally rang for.'

There is a malignant light in the pale-green eyes behind the spectacles.

'We shall see ... doctor. We shall see.'

And with that parting shot, the intemperate sister – the 'doctor' is nearer a spit than a word – withdraws. Dr Delfie remains staring after her for a second; then in one movement her hands come to her hips and she turns sharply. She stares down at her unconscious patient. Her next action is highly unmedical. Her right heel swings back and she gives the prone body a deliberate and sharp jab in the side, indeed with a force and precision that suggests she might be as good a footballer as she is a pugilist. The effect of this kick of life is instantaneous. Miles Green abruptly sits, holding the place that has just suffered, and with no appearance at all of having just emerged from a syncope.

'That hurt.'

'It was meant to. That was a foul, despicable trick.'

'I thought she was rather fun.'

She points angrily down. 'I rang for Nurse Cory.'

His face assumes a blandly innocent expression of surprise.

'But I thought Staff Sister was your idea.' Dr Delfie stares at him; then suddenly her heel swings back again, and he finds himself the recipient of an even more violent kick. This time he manages to parry its worst force. He clears his throat, and gives a winning little smile of confession. 'Just an impromptu notion.'

'Oh no it wasn't! She was line-perfect. You've been holding her up your sleeve ever since the beginning, in your usual ... it was a deliberate attempt to throw me.'

'You handled it jolly well.' He smiles, but she does not.

'And *Sister*. You needn't think I missed that, either.'

'Missed what?'

'That miserable real sister of mine.'

'Sheer coincidence.'

'Will you stop treating me like a cretin! Those spectacles didn't fool me for a moment. I'd know those wretched fish-green eyes a mile away. To say nothing of the ghastly holier-than-thou attitude. Always nosing round for dirt, what she calls dirt. Saying it's her moral duty, her obligation to history. Prurient old sow.'

'Honestly. I did have someone else in mind.'

'And as for that infantile and totally gratuitous bit of smut about my exposing myself to ... it's not just that you're so tasteless, so lacking in any sense of how lucky you are even to glimpse me, let alone be allowed to touch me, and as for ... it's hopeless. I give up.' She goes straight on. 'When I think of the hours and hours I've ... and over something that's ... I must be insane.' He opens his mouth to speak, but again she jumps on. 'It could have come to a perfectly happy ending twenty minutes ago.' He raises his hand gingerly to his jaw. 'Before that. When I asked to sit on your lap.'

'You only wanted to prove who's boss.'

'If you weren't so entirely tone-deaf to the subtler nuances of language you'd have noticed that I used the admittedly rather hackneyed and sentimental, but nonetheless in this context clearly signifying, at least in the linguistically sophisticated circles to which we are supposed to belong, expression "to kiss and cuddle".'

'I did notice.'

'When women say that they mean affection.' She stares darkly down at him. 'I don't think you'd recognize an olive-branch if you were sitting in a whole orchard of the things.'

He lies back on the old rose carpet, his arms crooked behind his head, and looks up at her.

'What your interesting stylistic run-down leaves out of account is that you deliberately chose a moment when you knew I would have to reject it.'

'I dispute that totally. All it was was a moment when you had to make a tiny leap of the imagination.'

'Through your hoop.'

She comes a step closer, and folds her arms over her tunic, staring fiercely down at him.

'Look, Miles, it's time we got one or two things straight. Since you so aptly compare yourself to a performing dog, all right, in the silly games part, all that nonsense, I let you off your lead. I know childish minds have to get rid of their aimless energy somehow. But the role-playing, the joking, the pretending I haven't even heard of Tzvetan Todorov and hermeneutics and diegesis and deconstructivism, all that's over now. When it comes to literary things that need true maturity and experience, like endings, I make the decisions. Is that clear?'

'Yes, doctor.'

'And you can spare me the sarcasm. I must remind you that you are an entirely chance and very transient biological eventlet and that –'

'A what?'

'You heard. A microscopic nothing, an amoebic drone, a lost bluebottle flying through the hall of eternity. Whereas I happen to be a female archetype with an archetypally good sense, developed over several millennia, of deeper values. On top of that you know as well as I do that my physical presence here is purely illusory, a mere epiphenomenon resulting from certain electro-chemical reactions taking place in your, if you really want to know, pathologically hypertrophied right cerebral lobe. Moreover –' she stops and takes a breath. 'Take your hand off my ankle.'

'I just wondered if archetypes had ankles.'

'If you move it one inch higher, I shall give you a much harder kick.'

He removes the hand. 'You were saying?'

'For all your only too palpable faults and inadequacies, I did have some faint hope that you might one day with my help grasp that the very least your selfish, arrogant and monotonously animal sex owes mine for all its past –'

'Please not that again.'

'Cruelties, is a little affection when we ask for it.'

'I.e., a screw.'

139

She stares down at him; then slowly reaches down a pointing finger, as if it were a pistol whose trigger she is about to press. Her voice is lower.

'Miles, I warn you. You're on the very edge of a precipice.'

'In that case I withdraw the colloquialism.'

'What did I say I wanted?'

'Affection. I'll remember next time.'

She folds her arms again, and looks across the room. 'As a matter of fact I came to a decision during that last scene. There's not going to be a next time.'

The cuckoo-clock ticks away in the silence provoked by this ukase. He begins to smile.

'Who says?'

'I say.'

'As you yourself have just informed me that you are not actually standing there, you are inside my head, I'm not at all clear how any decision about our future can lie with you alone.'

She throws him a sharp glance down. His eyes and mouth do not bother to conceal a smug amusement. But never, in the long history of the expression, can a smile have been so swiftly wiped from a face. One moment he quietly crows; the next he sits violently up, mouth open in astonishment. From sitting he kneels, groping wildly in the empty space that, two seconds before, she filled. She has entirely disappeared. He stands, hands once more desperately floundering through the air around him. He looks hastily round the room, crouches to look under the bed, then round the grey walls again.

'Oh Christ.'

He strides to the door and pulls it open: only, once more, to see the same room, blocked by his own bewildered face, the figure of his solitary double. He closes the door and leans back against it, staring at the bed. After a moment he raises his left hand, then impulsively pinches it with his right. Again he looks round the room. He gives up, swallows, clears his throat. His voice assumes a tone somewhere between a query and a cajoling.

'Erato ... darling?'

Silence.

'Bitch.'

Silence.

'It's not possible.'

'It's not only *not* not possible. It is.'

Her voice comes from the corner of the room where the table and chair stand, but it is disembodied. There is not one physical sign of her.

'Where are you, for God's sake?'

'Where I ought never to have left.'

'You can't do things like this. You talk about my breaking rules –'

'I should like to ask you something, Miles. Would you have treated me in the callous and barbaric way you have during this last hour or so if you'd known that instead of being who I am I was the daughter of a Mafia chief? If you knew I had only to pick up the phone and ring him to have a contract put out on you?'

'I want to know why I can't see you.'

'You've just had a minor brain aneurysm, or morbid dilation of an artery. It's unfortunately affected the ganglia between volition and mental visualization. They lie close to the cortex and are always rather prone to damage.'

Some new horror seems to strike him. He looks in agony towards the empty chair.

'I can't even remember what you look like.'

'Which will perhaps teach you not to meddle in fields about which you know nothing. Such as amnesia.'

He feels his way, almost as if he is suffering from a general blindness, to the end of the bed, and sits heavily there.

'Is it irreversible?'

'I am sure the entire literary community will join me in praying that it proves to be so.'

'You can't do this to me.' The voice is silent. He puts a hand under the mulberry-coloured bathrobe, over his heart. 'I feel faint.'

'You haven't answered my question.'

'I need a doctor.'

'I am a doctor.'

'A real doctor.'

'If you must know, Miles, the absurdly romantic role you and the neurotic rest of your kind have always attributed to me bears no relation at all to reality. As a matter of fact I was trained as a clinical psychologist. Who simply happens to have specialized in the mental illness that you, in your ignorance, call literature.'

'Mental illness!'

'Yes, Miles. Mental illness.'

'But what about –'

'To me you are simply someone obliged to act out a primal scene trauma. As usual it has left you with a marked feeling of destructive revenge. As usual you've tried to sublimate that by an equally marked tendency to voyeurism and exhibitionism. I've seen it ten thousand times. You also obey the usual pathology in attempting to master the unresolved trauma by repetitive indulgence in the quasi-regressive activities of writing and being published. I can tell you you'd be a much healthier person if you regressed fully and openly to the two underlying activities concerned.'

'Became a peeping tom and a flasher?'

'There is a profession that permits and even rewards those activities. In a slightly sublimated form.'

'What?'

'The theatrical, Miles. You should have been an actor or director. But I'm afraid it's too late for that now.'

'You wouldn't dare talk like this to my face.'

'That is because I am inevitably cast as a surrogate for your mother – in other words, as a chief target for your repressed feelings of Oedipal rejection, transmuted into *Rachsucht*, or need for revenge. I think it's time you reread Freud. Or another of my more gifted students, Fenichel. Try *The Psychoanalytic Theory of Neurosis*. New York. W. W. Norton and Company. 1945.'

'If Freud had ever met you, he'd have jumped into the Danube.'

'Don't be childish, Miles. You're merely confirming my diagnosis again.'

'What do you mean, again?'

'I don't think I have to gloss the true anaclitic purport behind your need to humiliate a woman doctor symbolically.' There is silence. Then suddenly her voice is much closer, beside the bed, just behind him. 'It was never really thunderbolts and tridents, you know. We've always believed, in my family, in letting nature cure nature.'

He sits with bowed head; but then without warning he twists and dives across the corner of the bed, in a kind of improvised rugby tackle, at where the voice seems to come from. Alas, his right knee catches the rather high corner of the hospital bed and despite a frantic clutch to save himself, he falls off it to the floor. He picks himself angrily up. Now the maddening voice comes from the top of the domed ceiling, above his head.

'I shouldn't worry. It won't prevent you leading a perfectly normal life. Very probably a far more useful one. As a road-digger, perhaps. Or a garbage-collector.'

He stares up. 'You'd better not appear again, by God.'

'I have no intention of appearing again. In fact in a very short while the aneurysm will spread to the related aural ganglia. You won't even hear my voice.'

He almost shouts at the ceiling.

'The sooner you piss off back to your bloody boring mountain, the happier I shall be!'

The vehemence of this declaration is somewhat spoilt by the direction of her answer: once more from the table in the corner.

'I haven't quite finished with you. First of all I'd like you to consider how lucky you are I didn't ask my father to make it a major brain haemorrhage. I'll pass over the whole matter of your sneering scepticism and your attempts to mock all I stand for. Given your very superficial level of intelligence, and the general clinical picture, I suppose I can hardly blame you for having been indoctrinated by the cheaply iconoclastic spirit of a talentless and self-destructive culture.'

'You enjoyed every minute of it.'

'No, Miles. If I gave that illusion, it was simply to test you. To see what depths you would descend to. In the vain hope that at some point you would cry, Enough, I tamper with sacred mysteries.'

'Christ, if I could just get my hands on you.'

'What I cannot forgive is your ingratitude. It is some time since I took such an interest in any of my patients, as I have in you. And as for the artistic side – I've done my best, against all natural inclination, to adapt myself to your ploddingly literal imagination. Now the whole episode is over I can tell you there was place after place where I was silently screaming for even the smallest sign of a veiling metaphor.'

'I shall murder you.'

'And what I want you to remember, when I'm finally

144

gone for ever, which will be any moment now, is how you've lost the chance of a lifetime. Instead of *this*, Miles, I might have been sitting on your lap. As a matter of fact I might very well have been having a little cry and making you feel all male and strong and the rest of it. Properly approached and wooed, I'm not in the least like that ridiculous caricature of a hag-ridden old puritan you quite unnecessarily dragged in. Your comforting caresses would have grown into erotic ones, I shouldn't have minded your taking advantage of my emotion, in circumstances like that it would have been perfectly plausible, and we might quite naturally have ended up in a mutually satisfying position. But making *love*, Miles, not that disgusting, mechanical term you employed. We should have been sweetly, forgivingly, passionately one. The whole episode would have closed on that, it would have redeemed all the stupidity of the rest. But here we are. When we could have been there – your proud manhood in deep possession of my abandoned femininity, masterfully provoking new tears, but this time of carnal bliss.'

'Jesus.'

'Our fused bodies in final togetherness, eternally awaiting climax.' The voice stops, as if belatedly aware that it has risen a shade too lyrically to its proposition; then goes on in a flatter tone. 'That's what you've destroyed. Made impossible for ever now.'

He looks grimly at where the voice came from. 'As I can't visualize you any more, I can't even imagine what I'm missing.' He adds, 'And as for eternally awaiting climax, it sounds more like constipation than anything else.'

'You're so unimaginably insensitive.'

Now he folds his arms, and once again eyes the empty chair, with a calculated cunning.

'I can still remember that black girl, you know.'

'I don't wish to talk about her. She was an extremely superfluous idea from the beginning.'

'And how she left you absolutely standing for looks. And sexiness.'

'How can you possibly tell? You've forgotten what I look like.'

'By a process of deduction. If she was this, you must have been that.'

'That does *not* follow at all.'

He leans back on an elbow. 'I can still feel her lovely rich brown skin, how warm and compact and voluptuously curved her body was. She was sensational.' He smiles at the empty chair in the corner. 'From which I'm afraid I have to conclude that you must have been rather fat and pasty-faced. Not your fault, of course. I'm sure psychiatry's an unhealthy profession.'

'I will not listen a moment more to –'

'And that mouth of hers. It was like jacaranda blossom. Yours must have tasted of Greek onions or something. It's all coming back, she gave off that wonderful feeling of really wanting it, no holds barred, anything goes. She was like great jazz. Bessie Smith, Billie Holiday ... I think the impression I must have got from you, whoever you are, was of a rather priggish fear of your own body, never being able to release, just one more intellectual cold fish, a standard female Wasp, far too frigid and generally screwed-up ever to –'

There is no visible hand, but the slap is real enough. He raises his own hand, and nurses the cheek.

'You did say clinical psychology?'

'I am also a woman. You pig!'

'I thought you'd gone.'

The voice comes from the door.

'I am just about to. But not before I tell you that you are

the most absurdly conceited man I've ever had dealings with. God, how *you* have the nerve to – the one thing you would-be strutting cocks of the universe have never registered about a liberated woman is that she can't be conned over sex. I wouldn't even put you in the top fifty thousand, just in this country, which everyone knows is the masculine bottom in bed – and quite literally. I could tell from the moment we first met. You'd have been far happier if I'd been a sailor or a choirboy.' There is a moment's silence. 'Black girl, that's a joke. Who do you seriously think you're talking to? Who do you think was the Dark Lady of the *Sonnets*, for a start? You name them, I've known them. And not just Shakespeare. Milton. Rochester. Shelley. The man who wrote *The Boudoir*. Keats. H. G. Wells.' The voice is silent again for a moment or two, then speaks with rather less passion. 'I even spent a wet afternoon once with T. S. Eliot.'

'Where was that?'

There is a brief hesitation. 'In London. It didn't work.'

'Why not?'

'This is totally irrelevant.' He says nothing. 'If you must know, for some absurd reason he got himself up as a house agent's clerk. With some ridiculous hat he'd borrowed from a textile millionaire. I was rather bored and tired, he frankly – never mind. In the end, flushed and undecided, he assaulted me once. Gave me one final patronizing kiss. As I'm sure you would if I gave you half a chance, which I'm not going to.'

'I do wish you'd think of writing your memoirs.'

'I can tell you one thing. If I ever did, it would be to tell the truth about people like you. If you really want to know why you're a sexual zero, and about as attractive as a basket of stale laundry, it's because, like all your type, you don't begin to understand the female mind. You think all we're good for is to swoon at your feet and open our –'

'Hang on.' He sits up. 'Only a few minutes ago you were –'

'Typical. That's exactly the sort of police-dossier argument my prude of an eldest sister brings up. If she felt this yesterday, she must still feel it today. What do you think liberation is about?'

'Not logic. That's for sure.'

'I knew you'd say that. Has it never occurred to your poor little male brain that logic, as you call it, is the mental equivalent of the chastity belt? Where do you think the world would have been if we'd all worn nothing but logic since the beginning? We'd still be creeping round that sickeningly dull garden. I bet he's your idea of a hero, that all-time wet drip. Driving his wife mad with domestic boredom. Not even allowing her to buy a few clothes now and then. Any woman could tell you what that serpent really stood for. He just wasn't up to the job.'

'If we could return to the particular case. A few minutes ago you –'

'I was trying to get it through your thick skull that I have not *just* become invisible to you, I have *always* been invisible to you. All you've ever seen in me is what you choose to see. And that's metaphorically no more than this.'

Most bizarrely, suspended in the air, some three feet from the door and five feet above the old rose carpet, appears a cocked little finger; but almost as soon as he sees it, it disappears again.

'I can think of another portion of your anatomy that would have summed you up a damned sight better. They called it *delta* in Ancient Greek.'

'That's disgustingly cheap.'

'And accurate.'

'I forbid you to say another word. You're just a degenerate tenth-rate hack. God, no wonder the *Times Literary Supplement* calls you an affront to serious English fiction.'

'I happen to regard that as one of the finest feathers in my cap.'

'You would. Since it's the only claim to distinction you have.'

There is a silence. He leans back and looks down at the bed.

'At least you've done one thing for me. I now realize that evolution was out of its already highly confused mind when it dragged women into it.'

'And you out of one of them.'

'For which you've played us every kind of mean, vindictive trick ever since.'

'Something you innocent, lily-white, notoriously non-violent men would know nothing about.'

'Until you taught us.'

'Don't stop. Feel free. The massed ranks of certified male paranoia are standing right behind you.'

He stretches a finger at the door. 'I'll tell you something else. If you were Cleopatra, your Cypriot aunt and Helen of Troy all rolled into one, and standing there now, I wouldn't touch you with a bargepole.'

'You needn't worry. I'd rather be raped by a band of orang-utans.'

'That doesn't surprise me one bit.'

'I've met some contemptible –'

'And poor bloody orang-utans.'

There is a silence.

'If you imagine for a moment that you're going to get away with this ... '

'And if you think I wouldn't rather be analphabetic than ever stuck in the same room with you again ...'

'If you crawled from here to eternity I'd never forgive you.'

'And if you crawled all the way back, nor would I.'

'I *hate* you.'

'Not half as much as I hate you.'

'Oh no you can't. I can hate as a woman.'

'Who can't hold the same idea in her head five minutes running.'

'Oh yes she can. With shits like you.'

Suddenly he smiles, puts his hands in the pockets of the bathrobe, and sits up again on the bed.

'I know your game, my dear woman.'

'Don't you *dare* call me your dear woman!'

'I know perfectly well why you've really gone invisible.' There is a silence. He makes a mocking little beckoning sign. 'Come on. You know you can't resist an apple. Even though you're only an archetype.' The silence continues, but at last the voice speaks curtly from the door.

'Why?'

'Because if you weren't invisible, I'd have you round' – he raises it – '*my* little finger again in less than five minutes.'

There is a moment's pregnant silence; and then there comes from the door a sound beyond the capacities of mere alphabet (Greek or English) to transcribe; an *urrgh* or *arrgh*, but at the same time both deeper and more high-pitched, of a throat being slowly cut, of a soul being scorched, of an endurance stretched beyond endurance, an agony beyond agony. It is close, and yet seems also to come from the furthest depths of the universe, from some ultimate and innermost core of animate being, and suffering, within it. To any third listener, especially to one familiar with the less happy theory of the nature of the cosmos, that is, that it must one day fall in on itself out of sheer horror at its own asininely repetitive futility, it must have seemed a deeply fitting, and indeed moving, noise. But the man on the bed in the grey-quilted room is clearly no more than rather cynically amused by this cross between a moan and a death-rattle that he has evoked.

What might then have followed ... but what does come is a much more banal sound, though completely unexpected. There is suddenly a whirring, a clicking of ratchets and escapements from the hitherto supposedly silenced cuckoo-clock on the wall in the corner. It is clearly premonitory, despite its distinctly absurd and busy length, of some major announcement. It comes at last, the little Swiss oracle from the wooden machine, and cries its miraculous message.

At the very first cuckoo, Dr Delfie is visible again. She stands in her white tunic by the door, her hands only an inch or two from where they have evidently been clasping her head in a frenzy of despair. But now already she is glancing at the clock in the corner with an expression of amazed delight, as a child might on hearing the end-of-lesson bell; by the second cuckoo she has turned to look at Miles Green, who has risen from the bed, and is impulsively reaching his hands towards her; by the third, the pair are respectively running and striding across the old rose carpet; and by a fourth cuckoo, had there been one, they are impacted in each other's arms.

'Oh darling.'
'My darling.'
'Darling.'
'Darling.'
'Darling.'
'Oh my darling.'

These somewhat cuckoo-like words and phrases lack the

pleasing rhythm and swiftness of the true and experienced voice in the clock; and take far longer to be said than to be read, since they come more like gasps for air than words, and from among a series of fevered, straining, seemingly insatiable kisses. At last she turns her head away, though the two bodies remain as tightly clinging, and speaks more coherently.

'I thought it had stopped.'

'I know.'

'Oh Miles, it seemed for ever.'

'I know ... I honestly didn't mean a single –'

'Darling, I know. It was all my fault.'

'I was just as bad.'

'No, you weren't.'

'Darling.'

'Oh darling.'

'I love you.'

'So do I.'

'For God's sake make the door vanish.'

'Yes, yes.'

She turns her head and looks back at it. The door vanishes; and once again they are kissing; then collapsing to the carpet.

'Oh you poor angel, look how big – no stop, let me, you'll tear the buttons.'

There is a silence.

'Oh you darling, you darling ... '

Another silence.

'You're such a monster, I love it when you ... '

Another silence. And now something else strange begins to happen, although the pair on the old rose carpet are too self-occupied to notice it. A stealthy opacity begins to suffuse the grey and quilted walls. It soon becomes apparent that they are rapidly and quite unaccountably losing texture and substance, all solidity. Instead of cloth and padding they become, as it were, a fog at dusk; and in, or through, this mist there now appear surreal shapes, movements, like shadows seen through heavily frosted glass; or like the murky oceanic depths, through the porthole of a bathysphere.

'Oh that's so nice. Do it again.'

Another silence.

'Oh Miles, I think I'm going to die.'

Another, and very brief, silence.

'No don't stop, don't stop ... '

If their eyes had only been open, they would have seen that the treacherous walls, in what seems a crescendo timed to their actions, have changed even further, into a now quite transparent plate glass, which bars nothing but sound. And horror of horrors, on all sides of this room become glass box, or oblong greenhouse, there now appear, in a night denied only by the dim light from within the room, broken phalanxes of the sick and their tenders: patients in dressing-gowns, nurses male and female, cleaners, porters, doctors, specialists, staff of all kinds: who on all but one side edge closer, until their first ranks press, ghostly faces outside an aquarium, against the transparent wall. And there they watch, with a sad and silent concupiscence, as the dispossessed contemplate the possessed; or the starving, at a restaurant window, the fed and feeding. The only thing private, still left sacrosanct, is the word. Not that words are now being sounded inside that room, but only broken fragments of alphabet.

Outside, a yard from where the door has been, stands the implacable and formidable figure of the bespectacled staff sister, on whose face appears neither hunger nor concupiscence, but merely some psychological corollary of the starch in her uniform. On every side the serried faces; but around her, an emptiness, as a drop of antiseptic in a culture dish will distance an otherwise spreading bacillus. No eyes seem more magnetized by what is being enacted. They watch with an intensity that glistens. Only once do they shift their gaze, to deliver malign and lightning glances at the walls of mute faces to left and right and opposite. So might an avaricious theatre manager size his house, or a brothel madam her night's clientele. She sees, as she threatened; but inside a mind that can only see, and never feel.

It is done; and now the oblivious pair lie slumped, in an unconscious reprise of their position after the first and clinical coupling; the patient on his back, his doctor lying half across him, her head couched on his shoulder; but on this occasion with their hands affectionately clasped, the fingers interlaced. The silent audience watch a few moments more, but then suddenly, as if bored by this immobility, this cessation of action, turn shufflingly away and recede into the limboic shadows. Only the sister stands firm. She folds her plump arms and remains staring, as if weaker souls may fade away, but she, she shall never fail in her duty to snoop, to judge, to hate and reprehend the flesh.

Too much, even for walls. With a hundred times the speed with which they have become clear, a reverse metamorphosis takes place. The sister is caught by surprise, stumbles forward, is glimpsed for a moment with her outraged, thwarted face and hands pressed against the clouding glass, as if she will break through rather than be thus baulked of her prey. In vain: in barely ten seconds the grey quilting, the warm walls of protective, if somewhat monotonously uniform, schoolgirl breasts have returned, after their temporary aberration, to their original state. All external is once again excluded.

IV

Deux beaux yeux n'ont qu'à parler.

Marivaux, *La Colonie*

By God she can do the talking. She has seen
more of the world than you and me, of course,
that's the secret of it.

Flann O'Brien, *At Swim-Two-Birds*
(*slightly adapted*)

Miles Green opens his eyes and stares up at the domed and cerebral ceiling, thinking not, if the truth be known and some shred of plausible male psychology preserved, of the eternally beautiful, passionate, granting and granted young Greek goddess he holds in his arms, but whether, if one was doing the unthinkable and trying to describe the ceiling of pendent grey breastlets in words, accuracy could justify the use of the distinctly rare word mocarabesque; which leads him to think of the Alhambra, and thence of Islam. He kisses the hair of the houri beside him.

'Darling, well done. That was interesting.'

She kisses his shoulder. 'For me too, darling.'

'Perhaps not quite the most interesting yet, but ... '

She kisses his shoulder again. 'Definite possibilities.'

'You were really super today in some of the rallies.'

'So were you, darling.'

'Seriously?'

'Your new backhand smash about paying me a fee.'

'Pure reflex.'

'It was sweet.' She kisses his shoulder. 'I adored it. I could have killed you on the spot.'

He smiles, staring at the ceiling, and draws her a shade closer.

'Clever Dr Delfie.'

'Clever Miles Green.'

'It was your idea.'

'I could never have brought it off alone, darling. I've been waiting all my life for someone like you.'

He kisses her hair. 'I still remember that evening so vividly. When you first came.'

'Do you, darling?'

'There I was, tapping away on that ridiculous typewriter.'

'Crossing out nine words in every ten.'

'Stuck with that wretched heroine.'

'Darling, she just wasn't me. I was only being cruel to be kind.'

He pats her back. 'Then there *you* were, in the flesh, sitting on the edge of my desk.'

'While you almost fell off your chair in surprise.'

'Who wouldn't. When a dazzling creature like you drops out of thin air. And then says she's come to make a proposition.'

She leans up on an elbow, grinning down at him.

'To which you said, Who the devil do you think you are?'

'I was a bit taken aback.'

'And when I told you, you said, Don't be absurd, I've never seen you in my life before.' She stoops and brushes the tip of his nose with her mouth. 'You were so funny.'

'I honestly couldn't believe it. Until you said you were sick to death of hiding behind imaginary women. Then I did begin to realize we were on the same wavelength.'

'Because you were equally sick of imagining them.'

He smiles up at her. 'You still do that bit beautifully. Great conviction.'

'It comes from the heart.'

He kisses the inside of her wrist. 'It was so marvellous to find someone who understood at last.'

She looks demurely down. 'Darling, who else, if not me?'

'How sick one gets of writing – and even sicker of being forced to publish it.'

She smiles tenderly at him, and prompts. 'And so . . .?'

'If we could only find some absolutely impossible . . . '

'Unwritable . . . '

'Unfinishable . . . '

'Unimaginable . . . '

'Endlessly revisable . . . '

'Text without words . . . '

'We could both be our real selves at last.'

She bends and kisses him. 'And finally?'

He stares at the ceiling, as if the splendid moment of ultimate discovery is present again.

'The curse of fiction.'

'Which is?'

'All those boring stretches between the sexy bits.' He looks into her eyes. 'That was the clincher for me. I knew we were made for each other then.'

She sinks against his shoulder again. 'I've forgotten what I did next.'

'You said, My God, then why are we waiting?'

'Oh Miles, I wasn't as shameless as that.'

'You jolly well were.'

'Darling, I hadn't been had as my real self for almost seventeen centuries. Ever since those beastly Christians. All those other writers I dragged in just now – they never got within a mile of the real me. You are truly the first since . . . I can't even remember his name. I just couldn't wait a minute more.' She sighs. 'Have you had that poor little ottoman mended?'

'I've kept it broken-legged as a memento.'

'Darling, how sweet of you.'

'The least I could do.'

She kisses his shoulder. For a moment or two they lie in

the closest silence, on the old rose carpet. Then he touches down the smooth-skinned back, warm ivory, to her waist and pulls her a little closer.

'I bet they did really.'

She shakes her head. 'I was always hiding behind someone else.'

'Like the Dark Lady.' He kisses her hair. 'You never mentioned that before.'

'It wasn't a very happy relationship, actually.'

'Be a sport. Give.'

She breathes out, half amused, half embarrassed.

'Miles, it's rather personal.'

'I'd never tell a soul.'

She hesitates a moment. 'Well ... I can tell you one thing. Whatever else he was, he was never the Swan of Avon.'

He turns in excited surprise. 'You don't mean he *was* Bacon, after all?'

'No, darling. I mean that the one remembrance of things past he never managed to summon up in his sessions of sweet silent thought was anything so elementary as a bath. That's why I came out of it seeming so stand-offish. I frankly found it about all I could face to be within shouting distance. I remember meeting him one day, he was wandering down Old Cheapside, slapping his bald head and saying the same line over and over again ... he couldn't think of one to follow it with. I jolly well yelled across the street, I was standing beside a lavender-girl for self-protection, and told him.'

'Which line was that?'

' "I grant I never saw a goddess go." '

'And what did you shout?'

' "The reason being, you have B.O." Or Elizabethan words to that effect.'

He grins at the ceiling. 'You're impossible.'

'They were all the same. If literary historians weren't so po-faced, they'd have long ago realized I had a very bad patch between the fall of the Roman Empire and the invention of internal plumbing.'

He leaves a little silence.

'If only I'd known from the beginning that the real you takes nothing seriously.'

Her hand slides down his stomach. 'Nothing?'

'Apart from that.'

She pinches the lip of his navel.

'I'm only being what you want me to be.'

'Then not your real self.'

'That is my real self.'

'Then you can tell me the truth about the Dark Lady.'

'Darling, you wouldn't have fancied her one bit. She was just like Nurse Cory.'

'Not literally – physically like Nurse Cory?'

'The spitting image. By a strange coincidence.'

Again he turns in acute surprise.

'Erato, you're not . . . you're not having me on?'

'Of course not, Miles.' She raises her eyes to meet his. 'I wish I was.'

He lets his head fall back and stares at the ceiling. 'My God. Black.'

'I thought we'd decided on a rich brown, darling.'

'And you didn't mind?'

She sighs. 'Darling, of course I was joking just now. About being in Old Cheapside. I was only something in his mind. It's just that the something in his mind is remarkably like a something in yours. The difference is that you won't leave it there – I don't mean you in particular, but everyone these days. Everything must be "real", or it doesn't exist. You know perfectly well the real "real me" is imaginary.

I'm only being real in your sense because you want me to be. That's what I meant a moment ago.'

'But you were the one who came and really sat on my desk in the first place.'

'Darling, I just wanted to see what being real was like. Naturally I had to choose someone to be real to. Equally naturally I chose you. That's all there is to it. Really.'

They lie in silence for a moment. Then he shifts slightly.

'Shall we go and lie on the bed now?'

'Of course, darling.'

She stands and pulls him up. They embrace tenderly, mouth to mouth, then go hand in hand and install themselves on the bed, in the same position, her head on his shoulder, his arm round her shoulder, her right leg raised across his. He speaks again.

'I've forgotten which unwritable variation that was.'

'The twenty-ninth.'

'I thought it was thirty.'

'No, darling. It's two after twenty-seven, and twenty-seven was the one when you made me ... ' she presses closer. 'You know. You wicked thing.'

'You mean when you made me make you ... '

'Shush.'

She kisses his shoulder. The clock ticks, contentedly gestating its next cuckoo. The man on the bed speaks to the ceiling.

'I'd never have believed it. The way we make it a little more impossible each time.'

'I told you. Ye of little faith.'

'I know you did, darling.' He slides a hand down the slim back and pats. 'You and Nurse Cory.'

She gently pinches his skin again. '*As* Nurse Cory.'

'You do her so well now. I keep forgetting you're the same person.' He kisses her hair beside him. 'Ever since that time she, I mean you – fantastic. No wonder old William ... when you go wild like that. And no wonder he went bald, if it was all going on in his head.'

'It really was, darling.'

He finds her right hand. They enlace fingers, and lie for a few moments in mute recollection. 'It's what seemed wrong today. I mean, only twice. We can't count the *interruptus*.' She says nothing. 'Our average is still three, isn't it?'

'Actually three point three recurring, darling.'

'Two isn't good enough.'

'We can make up for it.'

'It's the literary stuff. Each time we go long on that, we somehow lose sight of the basics.'

'Darling, I'm not disagreeing, but given who I am, I can't drop that completely.'

'My angel, I know you can't. It's just that ... '

'Just what, darling?'

He strokes her back. 'Actually I was thinking of one of your new variations today.' He pats. 'Of course you did it very competently, as always. But I couldn't help wondering if it was relevant.'

'Which variation was that?'

'When you pretended to be a psychoanalyst. All that nonsense about my being a voyeur and an exhibitionist. I frankly felt it was over the top. In the circumstances. And a wee bit below the belt. Especially the thing about mother-fixation.'

She leans up on an elbow. 'But Miles darling, who said only last time that he'd like to eat my breasts alive?'

'We surely don't have to draw far-fetched conclusions just because as Nurse Cory you happen to have a smashing pair of tits.'

'Only as Nurse Cory?'

'Of course not.' He gives a quick touch to the pair beside him. 'Both of you.'

'Miles, I distinctly heard. You said "as Nurse Cory".'

'A slip of the tongue.'

She looks down. 'I honestly can't see any difference at all.'

'Sweetheart, there virtually isn't.'

She looks up. 'What does "virtually" mean?'

'Only the tiniest nuance. And you can't be jealous of yourself. Just because as her you are a suspicion prouder and bolder. Even more sweetly impudent and provocative than you already are.' He reaches and pats the objects under discussion again. 'Yours are subtler. More delicate.' Once more she examines their delicate subtlety, but this time with a tinge of doubt. 'Let me give them a little kiss.'

She lies down in her previous position. 'It doesn't matter.'

'You are a vain thing.'

'I wish I'd never let you talk me into being a black girl now.'

'Darling, we agreed. I do need you in just one other shape – if only to remind myself how unconveyably heavenly you are in your own. Anyway, the point I'm trying to make is that, enjoyable though it may be to accuse me of incest and the rest, we surely have more important things to do. There were whole stretches today with hardly a whisper of sex. I sometimes feel we're losing all sense of priorities. We need to get back to the spirit of that absolutely marvellous time – which was it? – when we hardly said a word throughout.'

'Number eight.'

'That was so superbly structured, all solid, serious, nonstop – you know. We can't always rise to those heights, but even so.'

'I seem to remember I spent as much time being Nurse Cory as myself in that one as well.'

'Were you, darling? I'd completely forgotten.' He pats her back. 'How strange. I could have sworn it was all you.'

There is a silence. Erato lies against him. There is only one small change in her previous posture; now she lies with her eyes open. One might for a moment or two suspect that she is nursing a resentment. But that is soon proved illusory, because she turns her mouth once more and kisses the skin her head lies against.

'Darling, you're right. As always.'

'Darling, don't say that. Only sometimes.'

'It's just that I feel you're becoming so much better at being impossible than I am.'

'Nonsense.'

'It's true. I don't have your intuitive gift for ruining moods. It's not easy, when you've spent the rest of your life trying to do the opposite.'

'But you did marvellously today. You said things I thought I'd never forgive.'

She kisses his shoulder again, with a sigh. 'I tried.'

'You succeeded.'

She holds him a little closer. 'At least it shows how right I was to come to you in the beginning.'

'That's very generous of you, darling.'

She leaves a slight pause.

'Even though I've never really told you why.'

'Of course you have, darling. A dozen times, during our rest periods. How you've always admired my sensitivity over women, how you realized I had literary problems . . . all the rest of it.' She silently kisses his shoulder. He stares at the ceiling. 'You mean there was some other . . .?'

'It's nothing, darling.'

'Tell me.'

'You mustn't be offended.' She smoothes a hand across his chest. 'It's because I feel so close to you now. I hate having the smallest secret from you.'

'Come on. Tell me.'

She clings a little more. 'It's simply that I don't think you've ever quite realized how attractive what you call your literary problems always were ... are ... to a girl like me.' She brushes her fingers across his right nipple. 'I've never told you this, Miles, but I felt it the very first time we met. Of course you didn't know it was me, I was hidden inside whoever it was you were trying to imagine. But, darling, I was watching you all the time.'

'And?'

'Thank heavens, I thought, here at last was a boy who would never get it right, not in a thousand years, and already half knew it. All through your adolescent phase, when you kept battering your head against a brick wall, pushing out those ... darling, this is difficult, I *know* well-meant and you *were* doing your best, and I did try to help, but let's face it, hopelessly wild and inaccurate attempts to portray me – all through that for me truly *horrid* and frustrating period, I kept faith in you. Because I knew you'd see the light one day and realize it was as absurd as a one-legged person trying to be an Olympic athlete. And then at last this lovely, lovely secret thing between us could happen.' She breaks off, then gives a little sniff of amusement. 'You were so funny as staff sister. You do her better every time. I wanted to laugh out loud.' He says nothing. 'Miles, you know what I'm trying to say?'

'Yes. Perfectly.'

Something in his voice makes her lean up quickly again on an elbow and search his face anxiously. She reaches out a hand and caresses his cheek.

'Darling, people in love must be honest with each other.'

'I know.'

'You've just been absolutely frank about Nurse Cory's breasts. I'm only trying to reciprocate.'

'I realize.'

She pats his cheek.

'And you have always had such a rare talent for not being able to express yourself. That's so much more attractive and interesting than just being clever with words. I think you undervalue yourself terribly. People who know what they mean, and can say so, are ten a penny. Never having a real clue about either makes you almost unique.' She contemplates him with a tender solicitude. 'It really is why I came to you to be real, darling. Why I feel so safe with you. It's knowing that even if you ever did by any chance – which heaven forbid and I know you never would – welsh on our little deal and tried to write all this down, you couldn't do it, not once in a million years. As a matter of fact I did at one time consider other writers, but none gave me quite the rock-bottom feeling of security that you can.' She watches him a moment, then bends across him, her eyes brimming with sincerity, her mouth poised just over his. 'Miles, you know like this you can have me whenever you want' – she kisses his mouth – 'and however you want. And if it was the other thing, and you *could* write it all down, I just couldn't be with you at all. I'd have to go back to being a shadow on the brain-cell stairs, a boring old ghost in the machine, and I can't bear the thought of being only a thought to you.' She kisses him again, but this time her lips stay almost touching his. 'And you're much, much better at this sort of thing, anyway.'

A last and longer kiss, and she sinks back to her former position, cheek against his shoulder, right leg raised across his. He stares at the domed ceiling, then speaks.

'Just as a matter of contemporary fact, quite a lot of people –'

'Darling, I know. And I understand completely if you'd rather believe *them*.'

He takes a breath. 'I do think I'm entitled to point out that you yourself have never actually had to write a line in your life and you've no idea how damned –'

'Darling ... forgive me. There is one other tiny little secret I've been keeping from you.'

'What?'

'Well ... as a matter of *historical* fact, right at the beginning, for several centuries after the alphabet first came into being, my literary sisters and I had problems. You see, darling, it didn't actually catch on terribly fast. Of course we were all frightfully green still at inspiring. But it was almost as if everyone were blind or deaf. It was partly the ghastly Clio again. From the start she did what she's done ever since – sucked up to the people in power, the famous. She's a quite shameless snob, on top of everything else. And she'd sold practically all that lot on the idea that the alphabet was the inland revenue's best friend. That was the only way they could see it. Goody-goody, now we can nail the tribute-dodgers. All it was used for were those ridiculous lists of oxen and honey-pots and wine-jars and "Dear Sir, I am in receipt of your unsatisfactory clay tablet of the 10th ult." ... you know. So the rest of us had rather a brilliant idea. You mortals obviously needed an example, something to show you there was equally good money and all sorts of other perks in literary accounts as well as their boring old financial ones. So we agreed we'd each do a sample of our own thing, just to point the way. To cut a long story short, Miles, I did once scribble a little something down.'

'Which has conveniently disappeared, no doubt?'

'No, darling. I saw a copy in a bookshop only the other day.'

He stares at the ceiling. 'Tell me.'

'I wrote it under a pseudonym, of course. And it's lost its original title.'

'I'd like to know.'

'The original title? It's such a shame, it fitted my theme so well.' She leans up on an arm and looks down at him. 'Miles, of course it doesn't apply to you, but actually I called it *Men, Will They Ever Grow Up?*. Or just *Men*, for short. Don't you think that's clever?' He gives her brightly inquiring face a sideways stare. She looks down and runs a finger along his biceps. 'It wasn't perfect, by any means. I realize now I never made my basic message clear enough. I rather over-estimated my readers' intelligence, I'm afraid. Half of them still haven't grasped what it's about. Even today.'

He stares at the ceiling again.

'Just tell me the modern title.'

'Actually, darling, I've got yet another ghastly sister. She's just like Clio, another frightful snob. They always side together. Her name's Calliope, she's supposed to be in charge of epics. And her example was the most killingly dull thing you ever saw. Not a single bit of decent sex or a laugh from beginning to end. So just to put her silly nose out of joint I took one of her rotten hero characters, and wrote *Men* about him. To show his sort up for what they really are.'

'Will you please tell me the proper title.'

'Darling, I just have.'

'The one we know it by today.'

She begins drawing little circles on the sheet with a finger.

'Darling, I feel shy. I've never before told anyone it was

really by me. It was terribly primitive and naïve in many ways. I got all the places muddled up, for a start.'

'It had a lot of locations?'

She hesitates, still tracing the circles. 'It did actually.'

'So it was about a voyage?'

'I suppose sort of.'

'And I don't suppose for a single moment that by some extraordinary chance this voyage started just after the sack of Troy?'

'Darling, I'd really rather not say.'

'And is slightly better known as the *Odyssey*?'

She sits quickly up and away and covers her face in her hands.

'Oh God, Miles. How awful. You've guessed.'

He puts his hands beneath his head and stares up at the ceiling. She looks anxiously back at him, then impulsively turns and leans across his body.

'Darling, you mustn't feel jealous just because my one clumsy little attempt at writing has become a kind of fluke best-seller.'

He stares up into her concerned eyes. 'I thought this was meant to be our rest period.'

'Of course it is.'

'How you have the nerve to call me more impossible than you are ... and just because I make one small remark in passing about breasts ... it's absurd. Every classical scholar since scholarship began knows Homer was a man.'

She sinks abruptly down into her former position, against his shoulder.

'Oh Miles, I've hurt you.'

'Obviously he was a man. He was a genius. If you ask me, you're the one who's jealous.'

'I wish I'd never brought it up now.'

'I think it's a good thing you did. It just shows the

level your mind works at. If you'd ever actually read the damned thing, you'd have realized the only reason Ulysses went back to Ithaca is because he didn't know where the hell else to pick up another boat and crew. And Homer had his bloody wife's number, for a start. All that weaving bit. Everyone knows why female spiders fancy males.'

She clings. 'Miles, you're going to make me cry. Rather like Penelope, actually.'

He takes a breath. 'All right, he had to give her a certain kind of sloppy sentimentality. I suppose even then one had to throw some sort of bone to one's female readers.'

'Please don't say "female" as if it were a swearword. And please put your arm around me again.'

He does not move for a moment or two; but then does, with that quick understanding of feminine irrationality that so marks the masculine mind, take his right arm from beneath his head, and encircles her back again; a moment or two later still, he pats it.

'Okay. I'll believe you gave him one or two ideas. Circe and Calypso, and so on.'

She kisses his shoulder. 'Thank you, darling. That's very open-minded of you.'

They lie in silence, after this minor disagreement. But eventually he breaks it, though in a carefully neutral tone.

'We still haven't decided about next time.'

'Yes we have. Less talk. More action.'

'One place we might insert something is when you turn your head aside in that bored and disgusted manner and say, "I wish you'd just bang away".' He pauses. 'I thought perhaps next time I would.'

'It sounds delicious, darling. Would you like me to pretend to go on being bored and disgusted, or the reverse?'

'That's up to you.'

She clings. 'It doesn't matter about my stupid female feelings. I want what you want. You're the man.'

'You're supposed to be the immortal.'

'Darling, I truly don't mind.'

'I insist.'

'All right. I'll pretend to enjoy it.'

'I don't want you to *pretend* anything.'

She is silent a moment.

'I always know when you're angry with me.'

'I'm not angry with you in the least. It's merely that ... well, that all this does need organization. One can't improvise without forethought.'

'Yes, darling.'

'One doesn't sit down in a restaurant without having a look at the menu first and planning one's meal.'

'I know, Miles.'

'I'm simply saying that we do have some responsibility towards that three point three recurring.'

'Darling, I *know*.'

'Apart from anything else, you've got endless thousands of years more of this ahead of you. Whereas I –'

'Miles.'

He leaves a silence.

'We kept a steady four or five per variation up to ten. We've gone totally to pieces in the teens and twenties.'

'You *are* blaming me.'

'Absolutely not. Just a little more concentration. On both sides.' He goes on before she can speak. 'Apart from anything else, there are all sorts of ... narrative alternatives we haven't fully explored.'

'Such as?'

He stares at the ceiling. 'I thought I might take the initial treatment from Nurse Cory this next time. For instance.'

There is a silence. 'Miles, I can tell you as a woman myself that she –'

'I find it a shade odd that she was good enough for the greatest poet in world history, but apparently not good enough for me.'

'If you find a distinctly provincial someone else's brief *engouement* with a bit of brothel exotica shipped in from the Barbadoes four hundred years ago . . .' she breaks off. 'I realize I'm only a goddess.'

'You've just given her a whole new dimension for me. That's all.'

'I thought the old dimensions were quite enough.'

He leaves a silence.

'I'm not going to argue. It was merely an idea. If you're too grand to impersonate what seems to be a delightfully human and fun-loving member of an underprivileged race . . . there's no more to be said.'

Now it is Erato who leaves the silence.

'Just the initial treatment?'

'As a matter of fact we could make it . . .'

'Make it what?'

'It doesn't matter.'

'No, please say.'

'Well, it could be her throughout. I mean she could be you. A black muse again. Just to get the average up a bit.' She says nothing. 'It's not that I wouldn't miss you.'

'Do you have any other ideas, Miles?'

'Apart from suggesting that in future you wear slightly less hard-pointed shoes when you kick my defenceless body, no.'

A moment, then she leans up. Her face is once more all contrition, looking down at his.

'My poor sweet. I think it was just that you moved a tiny fraction, and I couldn't quite stop.'

'For the twenty-ninth time.'

'Oh Miles, I haven't! Show me where it is. Let me kiss it better.' He touches his lower ribs. She leans across and kisses the place better; then straightens and looks reproachfully down at him.

'Darling, you are so typically English, the way you bottle things up. Like Nurse Cory and her breasts.' She contemplates him for a reflective, though affectionate, moment. 'You do remind me of someone sometimes.'

'Who?'

'Just someone I met a long time ago.'

He gives her a suspicious look.

'Who?'

Still perched on an arm, she runs a hand gently down his chest, and makes a little smoothing circle round his navel.

'I can't even remember his name any more. He was nobody. I only met him once. Actually I had a friend I used to share with my jolly sister Thalia. Called Charlie. He took me along. Strictly for jokes.'

'Who was Charlie?'

'Let me cuddle up again.' She resumes her previous position. 'Mm, that's so nice. Charlie was ... oh God, my memory. If only there weren't so many of them.' She taps a hand on his shoulder; then a final tap of triumph. 'French.'

'This happened in France?'

'No, in Greece. Definitely in Greece.'

'But Charlie isn't –'

Her right hand moves to silence his mouth. 'Miles, I know. It's my absurd system. Wait a minute. French ... that's it! I knew I'd get there in the end. Brekekekex, coàx, coàx. One of Charlie's plays was about frogs.'

He stares at the ceiling. 'Why Charlie, for God's sake?'

'His real name's so long. I can never remember it.'

'We're in fifth-century Athens?'

'Darling, I couldn't swear to the date. But you're quite right, it *was* Athens, and long before the discos and Onassises and things like that. And so long ago you mustn't be jealous, but I really was terribly fond of Charlie, he was actually one of the only four Athenian men who weren't raging queers, there honestly wasn't much choice for a girl, and Thalia and I'd taken him a little idea for another play, with some quite nice female parts, which he developed rather brilliantly, though if I'm honest there was a crack about the women of Miletus that – but that's another story. Anyway. We trotted off to see old Doodah. He lived in a simply appalling ground-floor flat near the market-place, absolutely no light, it was more like a cave than a flat, and just to make things worse he was sitting at the back of it crouched over a fire … even though it was a sweltering day. You can't imagine. The silly old fool obviously couldn't be bothered with us, he hardly gave me a glance when Charlie introduced me. Of course I was there *incognito*, he didn't know who I was. Not that I think he'd have taken any notice even if he had. All he really seemed to want to do was hold his hand in front of the fire and make idiotic shadow-patterns on the wall. As if Charlie and I were four-year-olds. It's incredible, but apparently some kid had showed him how to make them only the day before. I could see at a glance he was nearly senile. He ought to have been in an old people's home. Am I boring you?'

He stares at the ceiling. 'Go on.'

'I mean, there is a limit to flapping birds and funny faces and wolf-heads. In the end Charlie and I got quite incredibly choked off with all of this, and just for a giggle Charlie suggested I took all my clothes off, I remember I was wearing a rather dinky little pale saffron number with a key-pattern frieze embroidered in red wool round the hem, it came from a darling Cephalonian boutique behind the Stoa, an amazing snip in a spring sale just the week before, straight off the rack and just my sort of chiton ... where was I?'

'About to take it off in front of –'

'You know, just to see what my naked shadow looked like and give the poor old doddering creep a thrill – and do you know what actually happened? He snatched up a broom by the fireplace and started quavering the most unspeakable insults at poor Charlie. That if Charlie thought one of his chorus-girl pick-ups – those were his very words – was his – old Doodah's – notion of the ideal woman he needed his vulgar little vaudeville head examined. Then he had the gall to tell me my nose was too long, my eyebrows weren't properly plucked, my divine little chiton was three inches too short, my arms and legs too thin, my bottom didn't stick out enough ... of course that last thing gave the game away. He was like all the rest. His real notion of an ideal woman was an ideal boy. Charlie told him so to his miserable face. If he hadn't jumped back he'd have got the broom across his head. We just had to run for it in the end. With old Doodah standing at his door and waving his wretched broom and shouting nonsense, how he'd have the guardians, God knows what he thought they were, after us for invasion of ... ' she pauses. 'He was a what-d'you-call-it.'

'Not a philosopher, by any chance?'

'How extraordinary. How did you ...'

'Just a guess.'

'I mean, that crowd are all the same. Charlie put it rather amusingly in one of his farces. He said they didn't know their *phalloi* from their *pyge*.'

'Which farce was that?'

'The horrid Clio once told me it hadn't survived. But

knowing her I expect she's just filed it under Inca irrigation systems or something. So she can sneak it away and give herself a spinster's Saturday night out when no one else is looking.'

He has continued staring at the ceiling.

'But I remind you of . . . old Doodah.'

She kisses his shoulder. 'Only very slightly, darling. A teeny-weeny bit. Just sometimes.'

'I don't see any connection at all, myself.'

'Miles, don't go all stiff and hurt. I'm not talking about physical things.'

'When have I ever complained about your taking your clothes off?'

'But you are always trying to turn me into something I'm not. As if you'd like me better if I was perfect. Or Nurse Cory. I feel I never quite live up to what you really want. I know I have faults. Actually my nose *is* a few millimetres too long.' She pauses. 'I had another friend once. He was always making fun of it. He was a rat, anyway. He went off with the deadly dull Calliope. I got my own back, though.'

'Who was this?'

'You don't mind me chattering on? You must say. Actually, I got "nose" stuck on to his real name. Then he was sent into exile. Where he wrote a most appallingly long-winded what's-it about the founding of . . . you know. March march march.'

'Rome?'

'Rome.'

He stares at the ceiling.

'You're confusing two people.'

'No I'm not. I couldn't ever forget him.'

'Virgil's the one who wrote about Rome.'

'Of course. How clever of you to remember.'

'The one you had an affair with was Ovid.'

There is a silence.

'Miles, are you absolutely sure?'

'Publius Ovidius *Naso*. Nose.'

'It does ring a sort of bell, now you mention it. Didn't I inspire him with some odes or something?'

'That was Horace, for God's sake.'

'Oh yes. That lovely little thing about a sparrow.'

'*Catullus*.'

'Oh I remember him. He was a darling, such fun to tease. I was his Livia, you know.'

'Lesbia. Christ.'

She clings a little closer. 'Darling, I'm sorry. I do try.'

'I just wonder if this is how you treat the great poets of the past, how the devil you treat –'

'Miles, I only inspire people. Sprinkle a few seeds. I can't be everywhere when the flowers come out. And reading anything but Greek always hurts my eyes so. No other alphabet has ever had quite the same undertones for me.'

Miles Green stares at the ceiling, and mulls in silence. She kisses his shoulder.

'Darling, tell me what you're thinking.'

'You know what I'm thinking.'

'Honestly.'

'I'm wondering if you've read a single line of anything I've ever written.'

Now she is silent a moment. Then she burrows her face in the side of his neck, and kisses it. 'Miles, I have read some reviews. And heard lots of people talking about your work.'

'But you haven't actually read it?'

'I know what it's about. The general drift.'

'I asked if you'd read it.'

'Well ... not quite in the literal sense, darling. I have always kept meaning to. Cross my heart.'

'Thanks.'

'Miles, you know I love the real you.'

'I wish you wouldn't use that word "real". You've totally undermined my confidence in it.' He goes on before she can speak. 'First of all you tell me I'm hopelessly wild and inaccurate. Then you reveal you haven't read a bloody line. You know something? You ought to take up reviewing.'

She buries her forehead against his shoulder. 'I'm like you. I'm not clever with words.'

'Look, Erato. The games we play in the game, so to speak, are one thing. But more and more you are introducing them into our rest periods. More and more you are making fun of things that are important to me. Like reality. And don't for God's sake tell me again that you're only being what I want. I do not want you like this. All you're being is what *you* want. And it's getting beyond a joke.'

'Please don't be angry.'

'I'm not. Just shocked. And extremely hurt.'

He stares at the ceiling. Her hand smoothes idly down over his stomach and finds his limp penis; strokes it, then squeezes it gently. After a while he speaks.

'You're always up to something.'

She kisses his shoulder. 'Which is more than you are.'

'I wasn't talking about that.'

'I can't help it over names. It's like having a cloud of flies buzzing in your brain.'

'Is that the best simile you can come up with?'

'What's wrong with it, darling?'

He keeps his mouth pressed grimly closed; but then can stand it no more.

'You can remember perfectly well. When you want to.'

She goes on fondling the penis.

'Some things.'

He leaves a small silence.

'It's all very well for you. Of course I realize that the thing in the meadow on Parnassus is only a metaphor, a symbol for the alphabetical conjunctions that make words, and so on. But I don't see why you can't make some allowance for my lack of sexual experience. Experience like yours. It's surely not too much to ask you to slip into someone else's skin for an hour or two. Once in a while.'

'Miles, I know black is beautiful, but it does hurt me the tiniest bit that I'm not enough for you as I am. Quite apart from the fact that we did agree in the beginning that I'd only be someone else when I felt like it.'

'Except that you never do.'

'I don't see why we can't simply be ourselves.'

'Because you don't understand me. I sometimes think we'd both be better off being two entirely different people.'

She raises the penis and lets it fall.

'Darling, I do. I may not have read your books, but I have read you. I know you by heart, almost.' Now she pats the penis, as if in farewell, and slips her hand up to his shoulder. 'And please don't let's talk any more. Let's have a little rest. Perhaps I'll feel different in a minute. When we start the next revision.'

'I don't consider this matter settled at all.'

'Darling.'

'All we ever do nowadays is talk. I've had you just a miserable twice in what would have been, if this wasn't an unwritable non-text, one hundred and eighty pages at least. That's not what we're here for.'

'I promise I'll think of something lovely for next time.'

He breathes out. 'It's just not good enough.'

'*Darling*.'

'All right.'

'I won't say a word. You can have me over and over and over again.'

'That *will* be the day.'

'I promise.'

She pats his shoulder. He opens his mouth, but then closes it.

Silence falls on the room, except for the quiet ticking of the cuckoo-clock. The two figures lie complected on the crepuscular bed, their eyes closed, a charming picture of sexual concord; clinging female, protective male, peace after the sensual storm. She raises her right leg an inch or two higher across his loins, and stirs her own sleepily against his hip; then lies still again.

All male sympathies must go to Miles Green; or so Miles Green himself overwhelmingly feels. It is surely not unreasonable that he might sometimes wish to tread (as it were) in the Bard's footsteps. And indeed he does, by way of self-consolation, for a minute or so review various mental slides of the vivacious, eager and now historically fascinating West Indian girl. But then he quite naturally elides, in the silence, to other solutions to his present predicament. Polynesian, Irish, Venezuelan, Lebanese, Balinese, Indian, Italian, Russian and various points between; shy, passionate, pert, cool; dressed and undressed, tamed and wild, chased and chasing; teasing, in tears, toying, tempestuous ... a whole United Nations of female eyes, mouths, breasts, legs, arms, loins, bottoms prettily slink and kaleidoscopically tumble through, or past, the windows of his mind; but alas, like the images in the fluttered pages of some magazine; or like snowflakes, frozen because unrealizable.

The maddening thing, of course, is that they all lie, waiting to spring or be sprung into charming life and labile reality, inside the body his right arm loosely holds – that is, if the wretched girl (Homer indeed) and her absurdly capricious and banal female vanity (particularly absurd in a family generally obsessed to the point of dottiness with showing how polymorphic they are) can only be brought to appropriate heel. It has to be said: like most divinities, she has picked up some rather silly human characteristics during her career. The way she goes on, one would think she was just an ordinary woman; even worse, a wife.

So reflects Miles Green. It is not, he tells himself with his usual objectivity, that day in, day out, taking all in all, the rough with the smooth, one can complain too much about having a goddess prepared to try almost anything (except metamorphosis and the Brazilian fork) as one's bed-partner; nor is that sole concession she has made to man's eternal quasi-spiritual quest for something a tactile centimetre (or syllable) better than what he already has, Nurse Cory, to be sneezed at. Nonetheless, one is bound to think of all the other concessions she might so easily have made, while she was about it. This has been the most bathetic revelation of all: the discovery that a muse might actually lack imagination in this matter has come as a severe disappointment. It is like being given a Ferrari, then not allowed to drive it over ten miles an hour.

He has to face it: if she wasn't who she was, one might reluctantly by now be beginning to wonder whether she wasn't in fact a distinct touch suburban. All this talk about being her 'real' self borders on the petty-bourgeois, on the dread disease cartlanditis, on the ethos of shop-girls. And as for being jealous of herself just because he begins to find her sexier when she is someone else ... words really fail him. One is perilously near demanding whether her true home is not Parnassus, but some vicarage.

Nor, heaven knows, is that the worst, thinks Miles. This last and intolerably wordy variation has confirmed only too well what he has long begun to suspect. The notion that the muses are shy and fugitive is one of the grossest deceptions ever perpetrated on man. For 'shy and fugitive' read 'irredeemably frivolous and devious' – and then you'd be a damned sight nearer the mark. The only thing the one beside him had ever slipped away from was anything that remotely suggested the serious. I mean (says Miles to himself), take a thing I might have raised and haven't yet but bloody well will next time – the little question of why ninety-nine per cent of everything this girl and her siblings are supposed to have inspired always has been and remains a total waste of ink and paper. It just shows how much they really care. 'Delphi Dancing Girls' was right; many a true word ... my God, he wouldn't mind betting the few that had produced something worthwhile had done so very much not because of, but in spite of Erato.

But what flagrantly gave her present game away was that she apparently could inspire, if she wanted to. She had been perfectly happy to be the Dark Lady, Lesbia, Calypso and heavens knows who else when she fancied; she had even been prepared to be a bit of a Grecian urn and a blessed damozel, for lack of anything better. But that was for other men; for him she is not even prepared to spend an off-duty session being a mere little West Indian nurse. On duty she has never even bothered to see what he might have done with a little grave and genuine inspiration, never even bothered to read what he had written in the past – when she would surely have realized at once that he was much too significant a person to deserve such dismissive treatment.

It has to be said again (says Miles): she is incorrigibly shallow, just as she is incorrigibly talkative. One might conceivably overlook the way she sends up everything one believes in in literature, including and not least oneself, in exchange for her passable enough body. But it is now shockingly clear that she doesn't even take *that* seriously. One can at a pinch allow two opinions about how respectfully one ought to take writing and writers; but not over what women owe men in the most fundamental thing of all. There must be a point, in that area, where the teasing and joking has to stop, and biological reality, why women are here in the first place, given its due. One doesn't want to boast, and one's certainly not going into competition with Casanova, Byron or Frank Harris; but one did not go to her, she came to one. And patently there can only be one reason for that.

This, of course, is what underlies her attitude: her resentment at being physically attracted to him – a crowning instance of how far she has fallen from true divinity and Descartes and how close she has become to being just one more brainwashed, average twentieth-century female. Heaven knows one knows the type well enough from the tedious monism of the real world outside the grey-quilted room: grudging, nagging, slighting, vinegar-tongued as soon as they think their precious little liberated egos are threatened by what their bodies have betrayed; asking for it, then denying it; slaves of their senses one moment, flaunting their supposed freedom of will the next; and always mocking what is beyond their comprehension, trying to drag men down to their own level. They are perpetually adolescent, that is the trouble; no sense of timing, not the faintest idea of when to stop, of when to be their age, as Erato herself so abundantly demonstrates.

Miles thinks back to their first variations – how physical, how passionate, how free of dialogue they were; how experimental, how sublimely irreproducible in text. And now! It is her fault entirely. With women one always ends in a bog of reality, alias words. From time to time one even asks oneself if they have not invented literature just to get

184

their own back, deliberately to confuse and to distract their masculine betters; to make them waste their vital intellectual aspirations and juices on mantissae* and trivia, mere shadows on walls. It could all be seen as a huge conspiracy, really; and who was at the heart of it? Who else but this totally slippery, malicious and two-faced creature beside him?

Miles Green should by now, it may seem, have been plunged into only too justifiable gloom. But in fact, as he lies there, there is something curiously like a smile playing round his lips. Its cause is simple. He has just set up, with great astuteness, a sacrificial pawn; and intends to lose it only to gain a queen. His recent reiterated references to Nurse Cory and her breasts were not in the least a mere result of tactlessness, or spite; but very deliberately made to outwit an opponent quite transparently determined to outwit him. When Erato is made jealous enough over Nurse Cory, he will spontaneously and lightly suggest she should be dropped – and then propose a new alternative. This new and far better candidate he has – not without a detailed review of all the possibilities, as already hinted – chosen. As a matter of fact he can't imagine how he was so stupid in the first place not to see how much more ideally suitable she was; and besides, having to impersonate her might teach the Greek girl (God, how right the Trojans were about charity from the Greeks) beside him one or two much needed lessons concerning proper comportment in the face of biological reality.

He evokes this new candidate now, as he stares at the ceiling. She is Japanese: modest and exquisitely subservient in kimono, exquisitely immodest and still subservient without it. But incomparably her greatest beauty and attraction

* Mantissa: 'An addition of comparatively small importance, especially to a literary effort or discourse.' Oxford English Dictionary

is linguistic. The very thought of it makes something inside Miles Green curl with ecstasy. With her, any dialogue but that of the flesh is magnificently impossible. One may just conceivably allow Erato, à la japonaise, a few sentences in broken English. 'Hallo, Johnny', 'You like a naughty Nippon lady', a few absurdities like that; but anything more will be splendidly and irrefragably implausible.

He sees her chastened and cast-down eyes as she kneels and tinkles away on her samisen – which can only be an improvement on the rifted lyre; then her eventually bared white body, smelling of rice-powder and chrysanthemum leaves, her glossy black hair unpinned, kneeling mutely beside him, her samurai, as she goes through some elaborate and increasingly delicious sexual equivalent of the tea ceremony. The fluttering hands, the seaweed-scented hair, the plump little Japanese breasts; and all in complete silence. Until, finally, maddened (he sees this most clearly of all), he throws her down on the tatami, or whatever the thing is called, and she lies at his feet, inviting whatever ultimate reward he chooses to bestow on her erotic skills. His infinitely compliant woman, true wax at last, dutiful and respectful, uncomplaining, admiring, and above all peerlessly dumb – except perhaps for one or two hoarse and incomprehensible whimpers of discreetly grateful oriental pleasure as her imperious lord and master . . .

Miles Green has, during this agreeable vision, closed his eyes. But now he opens them again. In some way, quite as incomprehensible as the Japanese whimpers that have just sounded in his right cerebral lobe, he feels as if he is swathed in towels; in either a Turkish bath or a fever.

'Erato?'

She murmurs, seemingly half-asleep. 'Darling?'

'Why's it getting so infernally hot in here?'

She pats his shoulder. 'Shush. We're resting.'

186

A few moments go by.

'I'm itching all over.'

'Never mind, darling.'

He raises a hand to scratch an acutely irritating sensation in his hair. The fingers alight. The next instant he has sat up as if he has touched not his body, but boiling water.

'Oh my Christ! God!'

The next instant again, with a superbly (in other circumstances) athletic spring, he has leapt clean off the bed and on to the old rose carpet beside it, and is staring in horror down his body. Erato has not opened her eyes.

She murmurs again. 'Is something wrong, darling?'

He makes a noise, not an answer: a sound neither as profound nor as universal as the one she had made some time previously in that room, yet similarly indicative of an outrage beyond words, beyond their transcription. As before, this heart-rending cry for help *in extremis* evokes no response in its cause; not even, this time, in the cuckoo-clock.

However, Erato does now open her dark brown eyes, and leans up on an elbow. She does not quite succeed in pressing the smile from her heavenly Greek mouth. If the lack of sympathy is monstrous, so also, it must be said, and more literally, is the appearance of the groaner; for what he stares wildly down at are his own legs and feet. The former are now strangely bowed, swollen-thighed and stringy-calved, and clothed in shaggy black hair; the latter are not feet any more, but cloven hooves. His hands claw desperately at his newly bearded face, then to the sharply pointed ears, then up to the forehead, where two stubby horns, each approximately one and three quarter inches long, sprout from the hairline. One of his hands (remarkably, he has not forgotten his classics) shoots round to feel the base of his spine for a horsetail; but it seems at least he is spared that. Small consolation: the pale North European skin is now so swarthy it is unrecognizable; and only by one or two facial features, had Miles Green but known, can any resemblance to Miles Green be detected. There is certainly no resemblance at all in the last detail of his anatomy, which now juts up and out to a prodigious length and size, tetrorchideously miles indeed beyond the dimensions of its predecessor in that place.

He looks, in a terrifying blend of shock and anger, at the smiling face on the bed.

'You treacherous bloody bitch!'

'But darling, this is what they called the anagnorisis. In ancient Greek. Besides, I thought you'd like to see what it was like to be me. For a change.'

'This is unforgivable!'

'And you did say I didn't understand the real you.'

'Change me back!'

She looks him up and down. 'It suits you. And besides, our average.'

'Will you change me back, damn you!'

'Actually I thought it would make a variation on the amnesia. This time you could be a severe case of satyriasis.'

'My God, you're asking for it!' She turns over on her stomach, props her chin in her hands, and smiles wordlessly round and up at him. 'You tasteless ... I didn't mean *that*!'

'We can omit the diphthongs. This first time.'

'My God.' He looks down at his ithyphallic self again. 'It's revolting.' He glares up at her, with all the revulsion of a lifelong teetotaller being offered a magnum of malt whisky. 'I don't know how you could even dream ... it just shows the kind of woman you really are.'

'Darling ... it's not that. It's simply that I'm interested in the alphabetical conjunctions that make words. Symbolically.'

He stares down at her smiling face. 'Okay. You've had your stupid joke. Now change me back. At once!' She bites her lips. He stabs a dark finger at her. 'I warn you. I shall write it down. Every damned word.'

Still smiling, watching his face, she begins, slowly, to recite the Greek alphabet.

'Alpha, beta, gamma ...'

'I'll make you the laughing-stock of ... I'll destroy every last illusion about you, I'll ... my God, I'll show you two can play this game.' He shouts. 'I mean it!'

She sinks on the pillow, her arms extended, as if she is lying in the sun, her eyes closed. But still the smiling mouth, turned sideways towards him on the pillow, goes on murmuring, as if remembering a long-lost summer's afternoon.

'... mu, nu, xi, omicron, pi ...'

'You'd better believe it!'

'... phi, chi, psi, omega.'

'Right. That's enough.'

She continues; or recommences.

'Alpha, beta, gamma, delta, epsilon ...'

'That's it.'

'Zeta, eta, theta, iota, kappa ...'

'I give you one more chance.'

'Lambda, mu, nu, nu was heavenly, xi was actually a bit much, omicron is self-explanatory, pi, rho ...'

'That is it. Definitely, conclusively, categorically, ultimately, terminally once and for all, *it*.'

'Sigma, tau ...'

'Every damned word!'

'Upsilon, phi ...'

'I'll never speak to you again as long as I live!'

'Chi, psi, omega.'

'I order you to leave my mind. At once!'

'Yes, darling. Alpha, beta ...'

How fortunate it is that the room is acoustically insulated. The poor satyr, goaded beyond endurance (even in satyrs), utters the most spine-chilling cry of frustrated rage ever to have emerged from a semi-human, semi-caprid throat. He stands, trembling. Then he makes a weird hopping spring and faces the door; and lowering his head, runs in a wild, scuttling charge straight at it. Fortunate, too, that it is so heavily quilted, for this furious tilt and final butt achieve nothing. The door stands firm. The man-goat merely reels back, not even stunned, only slightly dazed. Behind him on the bed may be heard the continuing murmur of the Greek alphabet. He turns and contemplates the snow-white and now slightly parted legs, the proffered cheeks, the cruppered back, the extended arms, the couched head, the glossy black hair. Glossy black hair! And in his nostrils, so much more sensitive than before, the unmistakable scent of seaweed, rice-powder and crushed chrysanthemum leaves!

'Chi, psi, omega.'

There is a second's silence. Then the creature on the bed raises herself a little and turns a blanched and doll-like Japanese face round to look back at his. It wears a hideously synthetic smile.

'Hallo, Johnny. You like naughty –'

This time there is no rage in his voice; only the primeval cry of the male, though not perhaps entirely without an undertone of the final shriek of the kamikaze pilot. With two rapid steps and a miraculous bound, almost in imitation of one of the chamois on the clock, Miles Green is airborne and sailing over the foot of the bed, reality found at last. But at the very last millisecond, in the apogee of his flight, just before the unerring descent on target, narrative performs its bitterest twist – or perhaps it is polymorphic Erato, with more delicate judgement and experience in these matters (and since it has become clear that even goddesses can be hurt), performing a hasty act of self-preservation. At any rate, in the tiny interstice of time between apogee and impact, her ephemeral Japanese avatar vanishes.

Implacably the fully armed satyr hits the suddenly empty sheet and mattress, like a jet coming down too fast on an aircraft carrier's flight-deck; and from which, deprived of any braking mechanism, he ricochets on as if from a trampoline. His horned head strikes with a sickening thud against the wall just above the bed. Perhaps it is less well quilted at this place. Certainly the clock must have felt a reverberation from the blow, for it starts without any warning, to cuckoo repeatedly. As for the satyr, this time he falls unconscious to the pillow. There, the last transformation takes place. The pale and motionless body lying face down on the bed is once more that of Miles Green.

There is a brief pause. Then out of nowhere appear two pairs of hands, one black, one white. The lifeless body is pulled round on its back. The sheet and light blanket are drawn over it and tucked in, tightly, on either side. The white hands float to the door and one rises to switch on the wall-lamp, a neat, rectangular, opaque white plastic panel, just high enough above the bed to have escaped demolition. Meanwhile a small black, or rich brown, fist gives Mr O'Brien's frantic cuckoo-clock a sharp tap on its side. It stops its cry. Then one hears Dr Delfie's brisk voice.

'Right, nurse. I think we've got time for a cup of tea now.' The voice changes tone imperceptibly. 'You will have it in my room.'

'Me?'

'You, nurse.'

'Thanks, doctor.'

The door is opened.

'Oh and I forgot. If you could first find a tape and bring it along. There's something I want to measure.'

'Curtains, doctor?'

'I think that more than probable, nurse.'

The door shuts. The delicate young brown hands fuss unnecessarily around the pillow. Then a West Indian voice, close above, speaks to itself.

'Curtains. The nerve. And she call *you* a racialist ... honest, Mr Green, this girl know more in her little toe-nail about men patients than that one do in her whole skinny white body. You jus' see if I don't, next time she turn her stuck-up back.'

The voice sounds from by the door.

'You ever meet that Mr Shakespeare, Mr Green, you ask him. You ask that man.'

The door closes again.

The oblivious patient lies on his hospital bed, staring in what must now be seen as his most characteristic position, blindly at the ceiling; conscious only of a luminous and infinite haze, as if he were floating, godlike, alpha and omega (and all between), over a sea of vapour. Merciful silence descends at last on the grey room; or would have done so, were it not that the bird in the clock, as if feeling not fully requited, as if obliged one last time to re-affirm its extraneity, its distance from all that has happened in that room, and its undying regard for its first and aestho-autogamous (*Keep the fun clean, said Shanahan*) owner; or as if dream-babbling of green Irish fields and mountain meadows, and of the sheer bliss of being able to shift all responsibility for one's progeny (to say nothing of having the last word), stirs, extrudes and cries an ultimate, soft and single, most strangely single, cuckoo.